THE DISTANCE OF TIME

by M L DAMM

RoseDog Books

PITTSBURGH, PENNSYLVANIA 15222

ISBN: 978-1-4349-9043-3
Library of Congress Control Number: 2007943844

Printed in the United States of America

First Printing

For information or to order additional books, please write:
RoseDog Books
701 Smithfield St.
Third Floor
Pittsburgh, PA 15222
U.S.A.
1-800-834-1803
Or visit our web site and
on-line bookstore at www.rosedogbookstore.com

DEDICATION

To all my family, especially L
Thank you

As the ship glides smoothly through the gentle waves, ghostly puffs of cool late-night breeze, feeling like lustrous silk against her skin, dance and play around Cathy's face and ankles. She leans heavily and very despondently against the railing.

She agonizes... leaning so hard against this railing could be my easy answer; all I'd have to do would be to lean a little further over.... Unnerving memories are strangling her, at times screaming, jump... jump... stop this torment...! But the quiet inner voice of her soul overrides the screams and states, I can't do that.

Moisture in her eyes puddles against her nose and slides slowly down either cheek. She wonders, why—why has fate put me on this deck, this ship, right now?

To a casual passerby, the woman's posture could seem to be a harmony in graceful mood and thought, but an inner turmoil is raging within her. She pulls the hooded cloak more tightly around herself.

Joe is here.

On this ship.

Here.

Now.

His presence felt in all the twittering, fickle, gentle breezes that engulf her, and agonize her.Close enough to hold in an embrace, and too far to reach.

Tonight she has recognized the man who opened her heart and poured immeasurable love into it for the first time so many years ago. But she knows, without a doubt, they can never have a life together, for she has seen his family with him.

She is alone. Devastated. Paralyzed with heart rending gladness and heart-breaking despair.

She recalls, in exquisite detail an almost daily diary of all the passions and feelings, all the joy of his kisses and his hand holding hers, and reluctantly her memory flashes back to when it all began—thirty years ago to be exact—she remembers, when she met him..

• • •

"May I take your order, please?"

The piercing electric blue eyes gazing up at her stunned her momentarily into a replica of a statue, her pen poised over the order book. She had never before felt such instant confusion; waitresses weren't supposed to get so easily flustered, were they?

"Cup of coffee, black, and Cosmo with the works, please," came to her ears in a pleasant rush of words.

She scribbled it onto the pad, walked over and put the order on the kitchen window turnstile, then turned to get his coffee and a glass of water.

The small booth he had chosen was in the middle of her working station. She had to go past it many times and she noticed this soldier with the sandy brown hair seemed almost completely at ease, only the light tap-tap-tap of the tips of the fingers of his right hand on the tabletop betrayed any unseen stress or nervousness. Glancing at him now and then as she went hurrying by, she observed his handsomely rugged face and easy smile and she sensed his blue eyes following her everywhere; once she turned from taking an order in the next booth, and his gaze was lingering on her. Cathy felt he was testing her, evaluating her, teasing her.

She stopped at his booth on her second go-round with the coffeepot, "Refill?"

"Yeh, thanks. It's good coffee." When the deep, husky sound emanated from his throat, she felt as well as heard the words this time. She looked at him with eyes bright and shining, and picked up the bare plate.

"Can I get you anything else? Cherry pie, or piece of cake?"

"No, thanks." He shook his head slightly.

He had smiled at her, seemingly tentative at first, but then more confidently and each time she caught his glance he responded with a quick smile as she moved back and forth among the booths. The straight-backed, square-shoulder bearing he projected very definitely had gotten her attention, and the few moments she had with him when serving his sandwich and refilling his coffee cup only piqued her interest.

What is it about this man that tantalizes me so? The army uniform he wears so grandly couldn't be a factor, Cathy mused. Or, could it? He wears that uniform with such—audacity, more so than any of the other military men I've met. A Master/Sergeant: three 'up' and three 'down' stripes on his sleeves, and all those hash marks must mean years of service. She had seen hundreds of uniforms in the hours put in at this restaurant, but other soldier's didn't have the self-confident attitude and air of authority this man did.

She couldn't help but think about him. She tingled at the base of her spine just speculating and turning thoughts over in her mind's eye. Was he married? Did he have a girl, or did he gather girls at every base? No, I don't think so. She had not specifically taken notice of his ring finger, but she somehow knew he wasn't any of these. She had observed a quiet, self-assured demeanor, rather than the loud braggadocio of many of the younger and less professional soldiers she had encountered.

Maybe that's the answer, she suddenly realized, his attitude, as though he could take care of anything, anywhere, and at any time. Stop it, she scolded herself; he's just another army man who comes and goes in this place and I'll never see him again.

But then, she recalled his eyes: clear blue, provocative and openly admiring of her. They had never seemed to leave her from the time he ordered his coffee and burger, yet, surprisingly, had never seemed intrusive to her.

She kept busy moving around her area, clearing dirty dishes, refilling water glasses and coffee cups, and serving the meals. Cathy served a lot of good food, the public having a wide choice of menu. The very large Cosmo-Burger on a huge, toasted, sesame-seeded bun—such as ordered by this soldier—was the specialty of the restaurant; include French fries and coleslaw and the customers loved them.

He didn't stay long after finishing his coffee.

She watched as he swiped his mouth with his napkin, threw some bills on the table, and walked to the cashier in the front.

She knew the Cosmos establishment was a favorite place for many of the soldiers in Colorado Springs to eat and relax. Downtown, next door to a theater and close to a few good bars, it was also near where the buses stopped to pick them up and drop them off from their bases.

Peach color on the walls made it warm and intimate. Enhanced only by white-shaded lamps hanging from long white cords dangling from the high white ceiling the only decorations were multiple green-leafed planters at the desk area, and also suspended here and there on the walls. Large booths were filed along the right wall and back wall, and others marched down the middle of the room with dividers to make them small and cozy. Friendly waitresses, such as Cathy, in their pink blouses, pink crown caps, and black taffeta skirt with two huge pockets in front, helped to charge that atmosphere. She always felt the restaurant drew the service people because of the warmth it radiated; it was surely a drastic change from what, she presumed, they were accustomed to at their bases. And the food was good.

Two hours went by quickly when she was busy. The theater next door had just let out and hungry and thirsty soldiers, some with dates, had settled into the light chocolate-brown leather seats. Gathering dirty dishes from her number six booth, Cathy caught a movement at the third booth of her section. Glancing over, her breath caught when she recognized him sitting so quietly by himself. He seemed almost noble and stately, his back not touching the support of the back of the booth, fingers lightly tapping a cadence on the tabletop.

Again? That's twice tonight. This G.I. must really be hungry. Her heart started a strange rhythm of knocking against her chest wall, her breathing suddenly felt as if she had been running hard against the wind.

"Coffee, black, and piece of coconut cream pie, please," he quietly ordered when she went to him. A grin lightly curled his lips, and his eyes danced with confidence now as he looked at her. He caught her eyes with his and held them, an eternity which passed in a silver moment in time; clear azure blue, penetrating, connecting, and she felt pulled—as a magnet lures—into them. She finally shook her head and jerked free, turned, and walked to the service counter with his order.

"Jill! Jill!" Cathy whispered to a coworker out of the side of her mouth as she nudged Jill with an elbow. "See the soldier in number three? This is the second time he's come in tonight, and he sits in my station. He is so... so... I don't know."

Jill glanced over her shoulder toward the man, than raised her eyebrows in approval. "He's gorgeous, Cath'. What's your problem? I should be so darn lucky!"

Cathy gave an annoyed shrug. She might have known Jill would approve; she liked all kind of men, but was still looking for the dreamy shining-knight-officer-on-the-white-horse; Always hopeful and optimistic.

Well, she thought as Jill went on her way, feed him, his order is ready. This sergeant probably works pretty hard, and besides, it's his stomach he's putting all of that into.

Cathy brought the pie to his table and watched him dive into it with enthusiasm. She shook her head in wonder, causing her shiny-brown wavy hair ensnaring the pink pointed cap to bounce slightly, a half-laugh of amusement on her face.

She was very busy and when she looked up he was gone.

Going to the booth, Cathy picked up the empty plate and appreciated that he had, again, left a generous tip.

Business had slowed around ten-thirty and the movie next door wouldn't be out until about eleven-thirty for the next expected rush of customers; time to clean each booth and refill the supplies: salt, pepper, sugar, napkins. She repeated the steps at all six, wiping each down in its entirety, and the edges of the tables where, when in a hurry, she didn't always take the time to do thoroughly.

A few customers trickled in and when finished with them, she took a well-deserved break at eleven-ten. She gratefully sat down in one of the divided booths, sipped on a soft drink, picked up a daily paper an earlier customer had left there and began to peruse it; the funnies, cartoons, obituary's, a column from a local journalist about the ski season and how slow it was this year for lack of snow, whatever caught her eye as she skimmed the pages.

She heard the question vaguely.

"Hi, there. If you're done with it, might I take a look at the movie listings in your paper?"

A pause in the sound of the voice. "Miss?"

She didn't realize the sound was directed to her, but then she heard it again.

A jaunty sound, "Hello, Cathy?" including a light rap on the partition between them. "Miss, if you're done with it, may I take a quick glance to see what movies are on now?"

She looked up from her story, startled at hearing her name, and he was sitting in the opposite section of her divided booth with a half-grin on his face, and a mischievous glint in his eyes as if pretending to be almost sorry to be disturbing her reading.

4

Startled, Cathy could only wonder, My goodness, he's here again! Third time tonight. Those eyes! Good thing I'm sitting down. They make me feel like I'm floating and all gravitational constraint is....

He interrupted her thoughts and asked pleasingly, his deep voice music to Cathy's hearing. "Might I take a look at what's at the theaters? Are there any good movies showing?"

Her hand shook weakly as she handed the paper to him across the divider. "I haven't seen that section yet, so don't know whether there are or not."

She sipped through the straw at her drink, suddenly nervous, her heart racing as she cast covert sideways glances at him as he read; No, no gold band on the left hand. Very sexy strong jaw, and his shoulders, oh, my! Very manly, and pulled back with definite military posture built into them.

Finally, he glanced up from the paper and directed to her, "Do you like Fred Astaire?"

"Sure, I love his movies, especially when he dances with Ginger Rogers; they can't be beat." She fiddled with the straw, swiping it lengthwise between her lips for the delicious flavor.

"Well, maybe I'm in luck; they're playing at the Rialto tomorrow night. Could I persuade you to join me?"

"I'm sorry, but it's Saturday night, our busiest night, and I'm scheduled to work. Maybe some other time?" Darn, I would have to be working. She dropped the straw back into the tall soda glass and pushed it down into the ice.

He persisted, "How about Sunday, do you have to work? It's still playing then." A grin crept quickly up the corners of his strong mouth and his eyes started to sparkle, shooting slivers of blue darts into her; she could feel them piercing her, and she was hard-pressed to speak, her voice suddenly quivery and shaky.

"No, I don't work Sunday." She softly replied, suddenly frightened at the strength of the attraction she felt.

He pressed his luck a little further, "Maybe you would prefer to go with another couple along? My buddy, Hank, has a girl he dates here. He could give her a call, and the four of us could go. Would you like that arrangement better?"

Before she could answer he was out of his seat, headed for the phone booth in the entryway, and in just a few minutes was back.

"Hank already has a date with Glenna Sunday night, and would really like it if we would join them. They're going out for dinner and a drink before the movie starts at 8:10."

He looked at her and his last words were not spoken in a question, but in the manner of a sergeant who was accustomed to being in charge, softened by a slight smile. "Would you say yes, please."

This strong, healthy looking, sharp soldier was different from all the others. He seemed so open and friendly and his eyes seemed to challenge her, yet caress her. She instinctively trusted him, liked him, and only a moment's hesitation passed before she decided to go with her strongest impulse.

Why not? She had not enjoyed too many dates she'd been on lately. Most were nice enough guys, but worked too hard at impressing her with where they had been, what they'd done.

Maybe the blue pools of this man's eyes hypnotized her.

They looked straight at her and into her as if he already knew all about her, more than she wanted him to know so quickly. But, curiously, she knew also about him, knew he was courteous, bold, handsome, and had a quality of attentiveness about him that drew her to him. There was an instinctive... something.... Her heartbeat quickened at the thought of spending time with...?

"My goodness, Sarge, I don't even know your name."

He immediately stood up, came around the corner of the booth and reached out a strong hand, a steely hand which cradled hers very gently. "I'm Joe Harmon, and your name is Cathy what?" as he nodded his head slightly toward the first name only name-badge.

Laughing lightly, she took his hand, "Cathy Cabal. And let me give you my address so you know where to pick me up."

Her hand tingled all the way up her arm at the contact made with him, and she reluctantly pulled it from his grasp to reach for the pad and pen in her pocket, then wrote quickly, "It's not too far from here; I sometimes walk when the night is nice. What time do you want me to be ready?"

"Six o'clock. That way we'll have some time before the movie for dinner. Have you been to the Grandview Restaurant on Colorado Boulevard? I've been there only once, a long time ago, and it's a pretty nice place. I think you'd really like it."

Hey, this guy knows how to pull the right cords. No one I've dated so far in this town could afford, or thought, to take me there. "Well, all right, sounds fun." She took a last draw through the straw in her drink, startling herself with its "sss-lling' sound as it drew more air than soda. Delighted, excited, and vibrating with anticipation, she said, "And now I've got to get back to work. I'm still on until one. See you Sunday evening then."

When she finished her shift, she caught a ride back to her apartment with Jill, the coworker who never stopped asking questions about the soldier all the way there.

"What's he like?"

"I just met him. I don't know, but he seems very nice."

Yeah, nice, sexy, dynamic.

"What rank of officer is he?"

"He's not. He's a sergeant, and my goodness, you've been in town long enough to be able to tell an officers' bars from sergeants' stripes by now, haven't you?" According to Jill's philosophy, time shouldn't be wasted with anyone below a Captains' bars, even though she hadn't learned to recognize them as yet.

Arriving at the front entrance of her apartment she quickly unlocked the door under the soft glow of the small lighted fixture on the ceiling of the porch overhang and slipped inside to a small foyer with polished hardwood floor. In the corner to her right a maidenhair fern sat on a pedestal stand; against the opposite wall she dropped her gloves and purse onto the small walnut table sitting beneath a round mirror with an ornately carved wooden frame around it, both of

6

which she had found on safari's at garage sales.

A few strides through the foyer she stepped up to a living area with rust-red carpet and casually styled furniture, and kicked her shoes in the general direction of the small couch with beige background and muted flowers, padding past in her nylon-clad feet, and, shrugging out of her coat turned around and tossed it with casual unceremony onto it. She chose to collapse, sighing a breath of relief this nights' work was done, into a plump overstuffed chair in a pale green baby-corduroy which sat at right angles to the couch. A glass-top coffee table was positioned in front of them. She made a mental note to mist, in the morning, both maidenhair ferns, the other one spreading itself on a pedestal silhouetted in front of a back window.

On either side her treasures of glass and porcelain figurines were placed on small shelves against the white wall; a light airy sprinkling of a few inexpensive prints of scenes and flowers were hung strategically, a few family portraits scattered among them. This made for a charming and comfortable on the eyes place that suited her.

Getting up with a sigh, she looked swiftly around for anything out of place, and decided, I better clean a little tomorrow: dust, shine, mop, polish; big date coming to my door Sunday night. Glancing quickly into the bedroom and bath to the right of the foyer, she went on in, picked up clothes strewn here and there, straightened the bookshelves and positioned the lamp back to the middle of the bedside table. Going to the opposite side of the apartment into the kitchen and tiny dining cove, she started humming the song of the day, Three Coins in the Fountain.

She thought about how the patrons had kept it playing on the jukebox all night, as she stowed glasses and cups from the draining board into the Cabinet.

I'm nervous about this date, she pondered. Why? What's so different about him? But I have to have this place shiny and 'spit-polished' if for no other reason than to show the army that a civilian can do it too. I've never worried about impressing a date this much before, why now? Oh, well, a shower, shampoo, and touchup manicure before I hit the sack will help calm me down. Hop to it!

An hour later, she snuggled under the cover of the bright and thick patchwork quilt her mom had insisted she take with her when starting out on her own. "In case your apartment doesn't have good heat, I wouldn't want you to catch cold." Bless her heart.

"It does feel good tonight, Mom," she sleepily admitted out loud. Her thoughts then drifted to Illinois and two younger brothers still in college there. Her father had died of cancer when Cathy was in high school, and she tried not to think of him too often; it still hurt too much.

Must be a lot colder in Illinois; February there is always more chilly than I like—brrr. She shivered, burrowing deeper under the comforter as the night enfolded her in its deep mystery of sleep.

She awakened to bright sunlight streaming into the bedroom bouncing wonderful light off the colorful quilt. It charged the room with rainbow hues, dancing on the white walls and ceiling as she moved and slowly awakened. Long hair fluffy and in disarray and eyes puffy from a heavy sleep, she shrugged into a pink chenille robe, stepped into warm slippers, and headed for the kitchen.

"I need coffee," she muttered grumpily, still not awake.

She filled the percolator with water, sat it on the counter, then dropped a slice of white bread into toaster.

Reaching up and into the cabinet, she fumbled through sleepy eyes for the coffee can and a mug. The sudden jarring ring of the phone made her jump, and the end of her sleeve caught the handle of the sugar bowl and tipped it over.

"Damn, just what I need!" she sputtered. "All over the stupid cabinet!"

Cathy had never been an easy morning person; waking up seemed to come hard for her. When she was fully awake she appreciated the beauty of brisk morning air and sunlight, but her first cup of coffee was very important to her.

She was still mumbling under her breath about 'mornings and getting up in them' as she reached for the—to her not yet awakened senses—obnoxious noise of the phone and picked it up.

"Hello," was growled in not the best of her manners as she reached over and plucked the hot bread from the toaster dropping it onto the countertop.

"Hi, I didn't wake you, did I?" came a somewhat unfamiliar, and yet enveloping, voice. "This is Joe, and I was wondering if you aren't doing any-thing if you'd like to take a drive? I know you have to work tonight, so we wouldn't be gone long. Maybe lunch at one of the little cafe's on the edge of town?" His voice came in an anxious rush as though he thought she might hang up on him.

Instantly she was wide awake. "How did you get my number? I don't remember giving it to you." She paused, but there was only silence on the other end. How did she know that she knew he was perfectly capable of finding her number by however means it would take?

Suddenly she was breathless, surprised, flattered, and only a bit annoyed he was calling. Which one was the prevalent emotion she couldn't say, each tum-bled back and forth, in and out within her.

She continued, "But yeah, I remember you from last night. Sergeant Harmon."

Surprised and flattered, she decided, yet somewhat confused. She managed, "And, yes, that sounds nice. It's nine-forty-five, and I'm not dressed yet. Give me until eleven-thirty and I'll be ready."

He gave a confirmation , "Okay", and hung up.

Mystified at herself, she replaced the phone on the hook.

What am I saying…why am I doing this…what kind of 'thing' is he doing to me that I'm going to be ready to jump when he calls?

And how did he get my number anyway, I'm not listed in the directory. Oh, shoot, I guess it doesn't matter now, just get ready.... I'll ask him later. She was perplexed, and strangely shaken. Slowly, methodically, she managed to clean up the sugary mess.

Since the phone call, her eyes, usually green-hued when feeling dreamily romantic and reading the romance novel of the day, were now transformed into darker, charged blue-grey that mirrored her intense bafflement at what had transpired. She was excited, flustered, and bewildered she could do this on the spur of the moment; usually, she liked a more methodical, slower pace of choosing with whom she went out with.

What to wear... what to wear....Going into the bedroom she pulled a light blue linen sheath dress with elbow length sleeve and scalloped neckline from the closet, shook it a little and laid it across the bed. She went back to retrieve black pumps, a small leather purse, and gloves. Was this ensemble suitable? Sure. Or would...? No, stop it! Put the things on and settle down.

But an impulse caught her, and she dropped her robe and nightie onto the floor. Turning back and forth, she studied herself in the tall cheval mirror.

In her mid-twenties and at an average height of five-foot-five, she had a slim, feminine figure, up-tilted round and firm breasts, and a tendency towards hippiness she had to constantly fight. She was good looking, her best feature being her hair; a wavy, golden-dark brown, combed straight back and hanging free. It fluffed onto her shoulders without a part, swinging loose and cut on a curve that shaped it a little longer in the back. A soft 'c' curl was smoothed against the left side of her forehead.

Her fresh wholesomeness only needed a boost now and then, and she used makeup sparingly. Her eyes were always friendly and warm, and this warmth radiated into her full sensitive lips and rounded cheeks. She had been content with her looks but now wished she were prettier, or even beautiful. Am I too proud? No, never really have considered what I might look like to someone else. But Joe? This sergeant must already like what he sees. Hmmmm.

Still twirling and twisting her torso and looking at herself critically, she frowned and curled her lips downward at the bruise painted on her outer right hip, earned when coming around a corner too fast at work and ramming into a low shelf jutting out at the kitchen service window. An impatience with herself caught her. Why now—why am I so conscious of how I look—why am I frittering around like this? Get busy!!

Finally, after a quick shower to help wake up, she was ready and dressed and just sitting down on the couch, when there was a knock on the door. Getting up slowly and going to the foyer, she looked through the small window in the middle of the door. Joe was standing there, and she took in a deep breath, ran her hands down her hips smoothing the sheath dress, then swung wide the door inviting him in.

He was magnificent in civvies. A breathtaking sculpture. A white shirt with flawless pointed collar showed off the wide grey/maroon stripe on a light grey tie; his steel-grey suit had an almost invisible deeper-grey stripe; a light tan overcoat was fashioned on his six-foot plus frame, and a brown hat was gripped in his hand; and an almost mirror polish was shining on his shoes. This attire seemed to make him another stranger until she looked into his eyes; orbs that hypnotized and drew her almost unwillingly into their power.

Those lakes of sky blue made her feel as if she were being inhaled, swirling helplessly into them very easily. She recognized them instantly. The sculpture was definitely alive and breathing.

Her eyes acknowledged Joe's handsome face. His short sandy brown hair was combed almost straight back from the left-sided part, and for some reason was having trouble staying in place in the slight breeze that was crossing the threshold, and he kept smoothing it back with the palm of his right hand. Solid muscular shoulders and powerful neck gave proof of his good looking, definitely military posture. His musky, masculine spicy aftershave drifted in to her, and she inhaled deeply of it.

"Hi, Cathy, glad you could make it." He gave her a very approving smile.

"After I talked to you this morning, a friend at the Blair Country Club called and invited me to lunch, and I thought you might like to go there. They're having their semi-annual membership drive, and the lunch rooms are opened to the public for two weekends and the week in-between. I've been there as a guest a couple of times. It's a nice place and not too crowded, has good food, and Mike will see to it we're taken care of." He took in a deep breath and his smile expanded. "No obligation to join, of course."

Just looking at him had activated all kinds of prickly feelings here and there on her skin, and a tingling sensation started at her knees working up and down her legs and into her spine.

His wide mouth, at this moment turned up into an almost impish grin, smiled with even white teeth. His high cheekbones—almost exotic in Indianesque structure—were punctuated with a slight dimple in the strong chiseled jaw, and was set off by a ruddy, tanned complexion; and the crinkle of his eyelids and light-brown lashes surrounding those liquid pools of blue couldn't help but turn her into a willing accomplice to wherever he would take her.

She returned a smile, "I'd like it very much as I've never been to a country club. How did you know?"

Laughing outright, a pleasantly deep sound that made Cathy shiver, he took her arm and escorted her to a dark blue Chevy sitting at the curb, handed her into the car, stepped around the front of the machine and came in on the driver's side. Starting the engine, he pulled smoothly into the street, took a right at the Main Street intersection five blocks away, picked up speed and headed south on the highway.

"Mike and I go a long way back. We joined the army together and spent many years in the same places in the same outfit. He knows I'm not a potential candidate for a membership, but he calls whenever they have these open-house days and I've always gotten a good lunch there. I think you'll enjoy it."

Cathy leaned back in the seat enjoying the ride. The air was cool, brisk and clear today with a slight wind blowing down off the mountains; add a bright, golden sunshine and the trip seemed almost surrealistic to her. Joe was still talking about the country club and Mike. "I don't play golf. Do you?" he was asking.

Shaking her head no, she turned to him a suddenly shy smile, and was afraid to speak because it all still seemed unreal for her to fully comprehend. She listened while he talked more of what he knew would be a good lunch.

"... and a drink, Do you object to having a highball or beer in the very early afternoon?"

"No, I don't think so," she smiled. "I've never had a liquor drink in the very early afternoon, or mid or later afternoon, as a matter of fact. But I'm willing to try it; sounds good even."

As that was being settled, he had turned into the long curved driveway leading to the front entrance of the club. A doorman in a bright wine-color, gold-ornamented uniform met them at the curb, opened her door, and helped her out onto the red brick paved patio leading to the steps.

Joe turned over his key to a valet and was handed a ticket stub with a number on it, and as soon as the valet ripped the car out of the space he joined her on the patio. Taking her arm he escorted her very chivalrously up the steps and headed to the coat-check window.

So, thought Cathy, this is what the inside of a country club is, as she casually looked around. I'm a little disappointed. I thought it would be more spacious and elegant somehow. It's nice... but....She glanced at the light brown carpeting with a small golden fleur-de-lis design that spread across the room. A two-foot border of varnished light oak strips of wood surrounded the edges to the wall. Small tables, and several chairs of deep brown leather were scattered at strategic spots, and a lot of—Cathy quickly counted seven—potted large trees and greenery here and there. A few golfing pictures on the wall. Nothing too impressive.

Joe helped her with her coat, and, shedding his own, handed both and his hat to the girl waiting behind the counter.

Slipping another ticket stub into a jacket pocket, he took Cathy's elbow and guided her toward the dining room.

Mike was standing near the reservation desk and glanced toward the movement that he had evidently caught in his peripheral vision. Joe waved to the tall darkish-haired man, and with a delighted grin spreading across his face, Mike pulled his dark-framed spectacles off, slipped them into a pocket, and came to meet them across the foyer.

He was nattily dressed in sharply creased khaki slacks, gold shirt, and a dark blue blazer with the club logo emblazoned in red and gold on the left breast pocket. As he walked toward them, Cathy noticed a distinctive limp to his gait, his right leg seeming to be stiff and uneasy.

"Hey, Joe, you made it! I was afraid you wouldn't." He greeted Joe warmly, extending a hand forward. Looking at Joe with raised brows Mike asked him to introduce Cathy with that glance, and when introductions were made, turned and stepped over to greet her in a warm and gracious manner.

"Hi, Cathy. May I call you that? It's nice to meet you."

As she carefully acknowledged Mike, she thought, I like this guy, too. He's a perfect type to be a club manager; a pleasant man who seems to have a warm personality and I already see why he and Joe are friends. I wonder what happened to his leg or hip?

Mike picked up two menu sheets, and taking both of them by an arm, putting one on each side of him, he chatted amiably, "It's so nice you both could come," and guided them to a table along the window-wall which overlooked a pond and the golf greens behind it. Pulling out a chair, he helped her to move into the table while Joe casually dropped into the seat across from her.

Professional, in charge, very courteous and attentive, she thought.

Cathy glanced appreciatively around her at the elegantly appointed table linens, crystal, and silver that was laid before her. Well now, this is really nice. More like I had imagined a 'club' would be. Cleverly designed groupings of pictures showing the club and greens at their best and most dramatic lighting were positioned across the room from where they were seated. Soft pale gold cushiony carpeting, off-white walls with borders of deep blue, cushioned chair seats in several pastel blue shades, white linen clothes and napkins with silver scrollwork encasing the crystal water glasses. Very sophisticated and exquisite in appeal.

"What would you like from the bar? Anything?" Mike asked.

"Sure, we'd like...." Joe hesitated, "What for you, Cathy—wine, beer, bar drink? What sounds good to you?"

"Just a glass of wine, please. I have to work tonight and wine will be enough, thank you."

Tilting his head a little, Mike inquired, "And where is it you work, Cathy?"

"Nowhere that is of any competition to this place, I assure you," she laughed. "A restaurant called Cosmos downtown. Ever hear of it?"

"Sure have," Mike replied, "I've been there. Good burgers and nice atmosphere, and," he winked at her, "the waitresses are pretty okay, too. That's where you two met, right? Come on, Joe, drinks are on me today. What kind of beer do you want? I have a really smooth draft most everyone seems to like. Draw one for you?"

At Joe's nod of approval, Mike placed the menus on the table, than was off to the bar telling one of the waitresses what to bring to them. Picking up a menu Cathy noticed with pleasure there were several good entree's to choose from.

"I'm going for the Chicken Pilaf. That sounds so good to me, and Thousand Island dressing on my salad," she confided to Joe.

When the waitress brought the drinks, Joe gave her the order for Cathy and included the same for himself, "...only Bleu cheese for my salad, please."

As she wrote it down and hurried off, Cathy couldn't help but notice out the huge window the golf duffers parading past. In their colorful knickers, shirts, and caps they were a kaleidoscope of color against the immaculate emerald-green grass.

Their wait was short, and, alongside their small salads, the waitress placed a small silver basket of crackers, and a ceramic bowl inside another silver carrier of three tiny scoops of different cheese spreads. Nestled in ice chips was another crystal bowl of icy cold radishes, celery, and carrot sticks to nibble on or dip into the spreads.

"Goodness, where are we supposed to put all of this?" Cathy smiled. "And we still have more to go."

Cathy knew she was making small talk, her thoughts were confused and keeping her from coming up with anything witty to say. She felt somewhat intimidated by the surroundings or by the man sitting across from her, she wasn't sure which, maybe both; mainly she was totally surprised to be sitting across from this stranger with whom she had come to this club.

Joe soon seemed to be more relaxed than when they first came in. Maybe the beer helped him a little, but Cathy hadn't experienced any relaxation yet from her wine. She channeled her thoughts back to her escort... He was saying?

"...and then Mike shipped back to the States at the end of his rehabilitation in Japan, and for a long while we missed him there. He used to get us the good food no one else could find."

Cathy asked, "I noticed he walked with a limp. Was his leg or hip injured?"

Joe replied, "He lost his right leg from infection from wounds." And by the curtness of his manner she knew that was all he wanted to say about it.

He had a knack for extracting information about her. She gave him a few tidbits of her—sometime tortuous, sometime hilarious—high school years, different places she had worked since then, and told him the basics about her family. While she discovered very little about him, he did confide, "My home is in suburban Philadelphia—born and raised; my parents still live there, and I have a brother, younger, and a sister, older." He continued, "I live only three blocks from where Grace Kelly's home is. I know her and we went to the same school. Hank, Mike, and I were part of the honor guard at her wedding. That was nerve wracking, and pretty exciting at the same time."

Cathy couldn't persuade him to talk about the army and what he did there. "Oh, that's boring stuff," he said. "But maybe you'd like to come to the NCO club sometime? My weekday evenings are free most nights, but I just can't leave the base."

They finished their lunch, and she drained the last drop of wine from the glass. It was all so very good. She never thought in their conversation to ask how he had gotten her phone number.

It was much later in their relationship, Cathy realized, in his profession, getting a phone number would be an easy task.

Ah, yes, the good food.... She didn't realize then, either, that Joe had also been talking about the good food Mike had procured for them in the prison camp. That was at the same time when he had told her they were taken prisoners-of-war on the Fourth of July.

An ironic date, isn't it?

•   •   •

Remembering that first unplanned date was as if she were living it all again, recalling it as though it had happened only last week. She shivered and lifted the cloak hood, pulling it closer around her face, and leaned more despondently on the railing.

CHAPTER TWO

Hank and Glenna were in the car when Joe stopped to pick her up for their Sunday night date, and after introductions he headed the car toward the Main Street intersection again, but this time the car was propelled north toward the mountains. The sun was low in the western sky, stabbing a glow of warming pink into the fleecy clouds that seemed to perpetually flutter around the Pike's Peak mountain top. The restaurant was located at the end of Colorado Boulevard, the road winding itself upwards onto a small foothill.

A valet took charge of the blue Chevy, and the four entered through wood-framed, etched-glass double doors into a large blue waiting room with dark blue brick tile on the floor.

Looking around, Cathy saw objects which appeared to be very old and fancifully made. There were several ornate chairs in a shiny golden upholstery placed at scattered locations along two walls. And as she walked by, she ran her hand along the lace tablecloth that spilled over the edges of a huge round pedestal table which dominated the middle of the room. All activity swirled past this noble table, and over it hung a multi-tiered crystal chandelier. Along other walls were four resplendently antique, glass-door lighted cabinets filled with beautiful Old-World crystal bowls, vases, goblets, and various colorful art pieces. A feeling of being in an ages-old castle predominated, and Cathy was mesmerized. Her eyes couldn't get enough of the beautiful pieces and she wanted to examine each one, her love of fine crystal and objects of art almost keeping her from joining the others as they were escorted to a table beside the window.

When they entered the room, the four stopped, gaping in amazement. From the spacious elongated room that straddled the edge of the foothill and built especially with the view in mind, was the beautiful panorama of the city. Deep-red velvet valances outlined only the top of the long high windows. The room was dressed in a deep claret carpeting, a golden scroll design swirling through it; high wingback chairs in red moiré tapestry with a suggestion of a flower pattern were snuggled up to small cozy tables. Two white carnations with fern sprigs stood in an etched glass bud vase in the middle of the pink linen tablecloth, a small red bowl sitting beside them with a tiny candle flame flickering inside. Black linen napkins were dropped onto their laps.

Crisscrossing the ceiling were large dark beams of wood, with burgundy velvet-like paper emblazoned with gold and silver streaks embellishing the resulting squares. This paper also slid on down to cover the walls.

There were no bright lights as it would have been almost overpowering, but the muted low glow in the recessed lights in the middle of some of the ceiling squares made it overall very peaceful and quiet. The room had a rosy glow to it as soft music emanated from somewhere they could not see. It brightened their mood, persuading them into a feeling of elegant refinement, and they automatically talked and laughed in low hushed tones. They could hear the soft clinking of silverware with the hum of voices and an occasional laugh would filter toward them.

The view of the city was magnetic, and they could not keep from casting their eyes into the glowing darkness. Some of the shimmering lights seemed to be stacked on top of each other in places where they were placed on a hill, and the—white or red—twin eyes of cars coming and going gave a colorful movement and rhythm to it all.

Darkness soon enclosed the top portion of their view, hiding the mountain and allowing it its mysteriousness, but starting to emerge to spy on that mystery were a few stars twinkling in their mischievous way.

Cathy couldn't remember what all they had talked about that evening. Everything, except the army, she does remember. It was as if it didn't exist for these two warriors, both of whom stated they were career men. It seemed at the time, for that dinner anyway, they wanted to forget it altogether. Her memories were of laughter and teasing, delicious food served with flair, and humming along with the music, at times letting the music fill spaces where talk was given over to the tasting of the meal before them. Two-and-one-half hours later, the movie long forgotten, they pulled themselves reluctantly away from the spell.

"How about an after dinner drink at Barney's?" Hank asked. "They have a good Crème-de-menthe ice cream drink that feels just right after a good dinner, and it's not far from here." Everyone agreed that sounded good, so Joe headed the car back in the direction from which they had come earlier.

After a short way he turned off the boulevard and edged into a side street for five or six blocks, then pulled up and parked along the curb.

It was a quiet street. There were a few closed shops lining the block on either side of the road. Leaving the car they walked across the street toward a huge multicolored and garish neon sign vertically aligned high above the doors and on the edge of the building that incorrectly flashed, "BA NEY'S", and then they could hear the music, very muted.

Barney's was a popular local tavern. Not many servicemen went there but the few who had found it, such as Hank and Joe, were welcomed gustily by the proprietor himself, Barney. The music once the door was swung open and they were inside was very loud, and with definite Western sounds emanating from the jukebox.

"Hey, there're my sergeant's," boomed a voice even the loud music could not diminish. Barney was headed toward the group with large outstretched arms and calling over his shoulder to, "Vera, get that booth ready. The sergeants are here and they have guests tonight."

Barney was once a sergeant too, in World War 11, "the big one", as he told them, and his friendly openness to anyone who is or was a sergeant helped keep some of his memories alive. He seemed to never tire of talking about the army he knew then and Joe and Hank even briefly talked some shop with him.

A pleasant hour, with lots of laughing and intermittent teasing from Barney, and the drink was good, not too thick but mushy and cold with the Crème-de-menthe leaving a nice minty taste in the mouth.

But Joe was increasingly unhappy with the loudness and constant barrage of music that was issuing from the jukebox.

"They all have this nasal thing, a twanging sound, and sounds to me as if someone is strangling them by the throat. This racket just kind of grates on me."

Hank had to voice his protest. "Hey, Harmon, you just don't appreciate a good sound when you hear it. I wish I could sing as well as some of these guys. I'd leave the army flat and take up residence in Nashville."

"Yeh, well, I've heard you in the shower, Dolen, and believe me, you can't. Even I can sing anything better than your imitation of..." was all the further Joe got. Laughing, Hank jestingly threw a slow curving fist at Joe. With a flick of his arm, Joe reached out, grabbed Hank's fist and pulled it lightly across the table, twisting it quickly and pinning it down on the tabletop.

"This is also a good way to get a new sound out of you, my good buddy," grinned Joe.

"Okay, okay, I give up. I promise I'll only sing when you're not around."

"Yeh? You've been saying that for as long as I've known you, and I know you won't keep that timeworn promise." They both were laughing and suddenly, sheepishly, came back to the realization of where they were.

Cathy indignantly interjected, "Why is it that everyone thinks only men can sing Western songs?"

"Yeh, Cathy," Glenna agreed. "There are a lot of good female singers out there. Just listen to 'em, Joe, they don't sound at all 'twangy'."

"Well, the women sound kind of strangled to me, too," Joe put in. "I guess it's because my ears hear it tinny and it just doesn't hit me right. I don't have a thing against any of them.

Some of the women are very pretty to watch, as long as I don't have to hear them. Some ballads are fine, but I like to listen to something that has a mellower sound to it and more orchestra, and not so much, 'He Did Me Wrong, Now I'm Crying the Blues' kind of thing."

Joe said he liked this place. Sometimes when he and Hank came here it was very quiet and cool and Barney always made them feel at-home comfortable. But tonight the patrons were keeping the jukebox alive and hot with the twang of cowboy songs and guitars.

They came to the conclusion they were never going to convert Joe to being a lover of Western music, and all were still smiling as they walked out of the bar waving a goodnight to Barney.

Laughing, joking, they decided to try another place, the Gringo Bar. It was closer to downtown, and had more of a Spanish theme to it. Hank and Glenna wanted to go there because it also had a dance floor.

The music, at times the very hot beat and passion of the rumba, samba, tango, and cha-cha, was fun to listen to. Most of what the combo played was of a temperate tempo that most people there could dance to, and the band understood that not many people could do justice to their special music, so a number of their dance sets were the popular songs playing on the radio waves and in the jukeboxes.

Hank and Glenna were exceptional and were out there immediately, twirling, gliding and turning, smiling at each other and sometimes holding each other very close.

Hank was dark brown eyes and deep dark brown, almost black wavy hair, cut short, army style. His frame wasn't as tall as Joe's, but he was also very wiry, muscular and lean, and apparently, from the way he danced, more loosely jointed. With a triangular face, a wide flaring nose and a mouth that seemed to be always in a grin, he was fun-loving, outgoing, and witty mischievous.

Glenna and he complimented each other. When she looked up to Hank from her five-foot two-inch small frame, her burnished copper hair cascaded to her shoulders, and her green Irish eyes teased and adored him. They both loved dancing but to her it was more.

She was a dancer with a local theatre group, small time, but to her it was the world, before Hank came along.

Joe seemed suddenly uncomfortable, sitting very quiet on the wooden chair, and looking everywhere in the room except Cathy. Was he brooding or bored, she couldn't tell.

Okay, Cathy thought, I'd like to dance...I think. Truth was, she loved to dance and was very good at it. She had a natural rhythm for music. Maybe it was an inherited thing, or possibly because her Mom was making music all her life on the piano, and Sundays as the church organist. Her mama had been a concert pianist in her youth, and had given it up when she married Cathy's father. But her love of, especially ragtime, and Chopin and the Strauss waltzes never left her, and she had played the piano at home whenever she could.

Cathy never acquired a talent for the piano. Her gift was vocal, singing in all the school choirs, at church, and weddings and other celebrations when she was asked. She even won a singing contest in high school her senior year.

Her hesitation of whether or not she wanted to dance with Joe was, what? Shyness all of a sudden? No, it was inwardly, and excitedly, knowing that when Joe's arms were to ever go around her, she would be captivated, bewitched, and never the same.

Is Joe feeling the same way? Or is he sorry we came here? Doesn't he like to dance, is that why he keeps avoiding my eyes? I know he's a brave man, so why doesn't he ask me to dance? Come on, soldier, she mentally stamped her foot, I want your arms around me. I want to dance!

But she waited, almost patiently, while both admired a few jumping, fast-moving dancers on the dance floor; both laughing at some of the antics of one couples' desire to show off.

Hank and Glenna came and went a couple of times, and the combo used their talents to spotlight their native music for a song or two; thumping music, fast and furiously paced with a rhythm that made you bounce and jump in your chair.

Hank asked, "Glenna, do you mind if I ask Cathy to dance on this nice slow foxtrot?" He held out his hand to Cathy, took it with a side glance at Joe and led her to the dance floor.

"Sure, go ahead," was her cheerful reply. "Maybe I can persuade Joe to dance with me. How about it soldier, are you game?" She nodded toward the dance floor, "this is a very slow dance, and I won't bite, I promise."

Cathy jumped at the chance. Joe reluctantly relinquished his place of security behind the table and allowed Glenna to lead him onto the floor. She heard him mildly protest that he wasn't a very good dancer.

"Pooh, anyone can just stand there and shuffle the feet. That's about all there is to it, you know," she retorted.

The two couples smiled at each other as they moved. And then, before Cathy realized what was happening, Hank had released her and pulled an unresisting Joe into his place, and he then took the vacated spot with his Glenna. Joe's right arm went around Cathy shakily and she felt his hand lightly pressing her back. A shiver went through her. Had she seen Glenna give Joe a light shove?

When taking her right hand in his left he looked at her somewhat apologetically, and took a deep breath. "I'm not a good dancer."

"That's all right, there's not too much you need to move, except to shuffle your feet a little," she resounded Glenna's words. "You're doing great."

Oh, my! Her heart was racing as well as her thoughts. The touch of the lean hardness of his shoulder was sizzling her skin where it rested on him, the hair from elbow to wrist bristling.

His hand nestling her fingers was sending electric shockwaves to her whole being. He was rigid, and, well, military-like, almost in a parade strut.

They smiled stiffly and moved slowly with the rest of the crowd, but she was unable to talk. Cathy felt a sensation of dancing among clouds, and it was too new, too strong, too delicious, to spoil by coy or inane banter. And besides, she felt a sympathy to Joe's methodical and self-conscious counting with a bobbing head—but to himself—the dance steps he was valiantly attempting. Joe must have mastered many things in his army training, but evidently dancing was not one of them. He had grace and power, but she had discovered in him a sweet gentle shyness.

Too soon the music ended and they were headed back to the table. Did Hank and Glenna plan this? She couldn't help but wonder as she noticed Joe giving Hank a friendly 'wait 'til we get back to base' kind of look. They had joshed good naturedly back and forth earlier at Barney's how Joe outranked Hank, slightly, but Hank had taken Joe by surprise.

And Hank was loving it all, his roguish grin and dark eyes flirting with Glenna. Hank must have known of Joe's uncertainty when it came to dancing, and he had pushed him to do what he would not have done on his own; he had dared Joe to enjoy what Cathy suspected he and Glenna had conspired on.

Halfway back to their table, a foursome who had just come in spotted Joe and, artfully dodging their way between the tables and people, managed to arrive laughing and loudly greeting everyone. They were two sergeants from Joe's company and their dates, who were out on the town having a great time.

Introductions were made, and an invitation given by Joe to join the group. They decided to connect two tables together, and, with the waiters' help, managed to get everyone seated.

Terry and Cindy, Dan and Julie were celebrating Cindy's birthday and hitting about all the bars they could find, imbibing very happily in each. Terry started immediately to regal everyone with stories, some funny and very raucously told, some not, and the more he drank, the more raunchy they were becoming.

Between the times of dancing, than singing Happy Birthday to Cindy over and over, his jingles were beginning to be very brazen, risqué, and tiresome.

He was sitting across from Joe, with Cindy facing Cathy at the one table, while Hank and Glenna were across from the other two when he started the ditty of:

"There once was a soldier who loved his truck,

He also loved.... "

Cr-a-a-a-ck!! A hand slammed down hard on the table in front of Terry and the limerick was never finished. Terry jumped, his eyes popped wide and his jaw dropped slack, and inhaling a big breath stammered, "Umm…er, I don't believe I remember that one. Come on, Cindy, time to dance again." And they were gone from the table in a flash.

Cathy had also jumped, and, very startled at seeing Joe's hand where it had landed on the table, turned, glancing quizzically at him. His eyes were like hardened dark-blue steel, his head still moving slowly in the very slightest perceptible movement from side to side in the 'no' motion, jaw clamped tight, and muscles rippling in his cheeks.

Cathy couldn't comprehend for several seconds what had happened, and then she remembered the words Terry was saying.

"There once was... loved his truck, Also loved...." Oh, for Pete's sake, how had it gotten to that kind of limerick?

Terry must have realized immediately he was about to overstep some boundary at the unexpected interruption from Joe during his recital, and knew Joe was not going to allow it. He evidently was treading on dangerous ground with his rhyme but did stop just short of trespassing.

Maybe he had had too much to drink and forgot about some unwritten rule Cathy didn't know about. It was only after several seconds of studious glaring at Terry's profile on the dance floor, and a few deep breaths, that Joe could bring himself back to what was being said at the table. Cathy almost felt sorry for the hapless sergeant and what the morrow might bring.

Or would Joe forget it since Terry did stop before he went too far? She suspected Joe could be a formidable person to have as an enemy.

Soon after Terry's small blunder the four went their own merry way. The others closed the Gringo at one in the morning, and decided to go for coffee before heading home, and found a little cafe further down the boulevard.

They lingered over their hot brew. "Are you hungry, Cathy?" Joe inquired quietly. "A piece of pie?"

"No, but thanks, coffee is enough," Cathy returned. "But you go ahead if you want something, please do."

"Don't believe so. Anybody want anything else?"

They talked and relived the evening, and too soon while stifling a yawn, Glenna had to confess, "I sure hate to see this night end, but I had better be getting home."

Reluctantly, they left the coffee shop, and headed the blue Chevy, very slowly now, towards Cathy's apartment. Hank and Glenna were wrapped up in each other in the back seat long before they had arrived, and Joe, glancing back at them with a smile and amusement in his eyes, threw over his shoulder, "Next time you drive, Dolen."

As she stepped out, he took her arm and silently they walked toward the door, breathing deeply the fresh cold night air and raising their eyes to look at the stars.

"Thank you, Joe," she whispered at the door. "I've had a wonderful evening." She turned to give him her hand, and her heart was racing as Joe took both of her hands in his.

"When are you off work again, can we go out?" Joe asked.

"As a matter of fact, I'm off tonight, too."

Joe seemed delighted as a smile lit up his face. "Is there any way you can come to the NCO club tonight? Can you get a car?"

"I think so, if I can bring along a friend," Cathy said. "Maybe I can talk Jill into coming. She's off tonight also."

"Heck, yes," Joe teased. "Bring all the friends—female, that is—you want. There will be plenty of company for them."

"But," the ever practical Cathy said, "Maybe you had better give me a number I can call, in case I can't make it, if Jill already has plans." With that in mind they stepped inside to the foyer, and Cathy found a pad and pencil for him in the drawer of the little walnut table.

"This is the club number," he wrote. "I'm usually there after 6:30 in the evening, and this is the directions how to get there." As he handed it back to her he added softly, "Come anytime then."

In all of this exchange, Cathy's heart never stopped it's faster cadence. But Joe took her hands in his again, leaned over, kissed her with a feather touch on the cheek, turned and walked through the door and down the sidewalk to the car.

• • •

Cathy could literally feel that kiss right now, fluttering and soft, and reaching up her hand she found a wisp of her hair has slipped from underneath her cloak hood and is caressing her cheek.

Coincidence or not, tears well up in her eyes at the remembrance of that burning flame he had started there.

CHAPTER THREE

When she awakened later that Monday morning, she had to shake herself to see if she was still dreaming or not. No... she seemed to be awake, but did last night actually happen? She felt her cheek and knew that it had, his kiss still lingering there.

I'd better get on the phone to Jill right away and see if she's free, she thought. Be just my luck she has a date or something else going on. Struggling with her not totally awakened mind, she headed for the kitchen phone. Impatiently, she waited through four, then six rings of the phone on the other end. "Come, on, Jill, answer the damn phone please! Be there…be there!"

Finally on the eighth ring, just as she was dejectedly starting the phone back down onto its hook, the sleepy, hoarse, voice of a man answered.

"H'ulo?"

Taken aback, Cathy started to apologize, stammering into the mouthpiece, "I'm sorry, but I thought I was calling Jill Howard's apartment. I must have dialed wrong."

"Hold on, hold on," came the muffled voice again, interrupting her, "This is Jill's apartment. Hey, Jill, telephone."

There was a giggle on the other end, and Jill's soft, sleepy-sounding, "Hello?"

"Jill, this is Cathy. Are you busy tonight or have a date or, umm, anything?"

Laughing lightly, Jill explained that she did have a friend over for last night, but he was getting ready to leave, and, "What do you have in mind, Cath'?"

"Well, we have an invitation to go to the base NCO club tonight. Are you interested?"

Jill inquired, "Just what is an 'NCO' club, Cath, a dance place?"

"No, silly. It stands for, I believe, sergeants and lower ranking than an officer, 'Non-Commissioned-Officer'. Would you go please please please, Jill, for me? I have no other way to get there."

Without hesitation, Jill said, "Sure. What time, Cath?"

Having settled on 'about 6:45 to leave my house', Cathy put the coffee on and decided to do the cleaning that didn't get done over the weekend. Scrubbing, polishing, mopping, and dusting seemed to settle her down, the vigorous activity an outlet for her energy. But all the while she kept thinking of, and reliving, the night before. She was glad now he hadn't kissed her goodnight like she thought might happen; this way she could get to know him better without that close involvement...but it wasn't that she hadn't wanted him to kiss her, that's for sure.

Humming and whistling to her work, she managed to get it all finished within a two-hour span. When all the mops, pails, and cloths were put away, she decided to take a long walk, as it was another beautiful, cold crispy day, and taking a turn around a couple of blocks gave her rosy cheeks. Arriving back at the apartment, she felt invigorated and fully re-energized.

Time to start getting ready. I think I'm going to take a nice long, hot, bubble bath instead of a shower, and take my time, too, she reflected. But she was too 'up' to stay for long in the bubbly cloud, and was soon toweling herself off, then lotioning and powdering. Curling her hair and putting on her hint of make-up was also finished in a very short time.

She had eaten a light meal and was ready long before the appointed time of Jill picking her up, and kept watch out the window impatiently. The toe of her black pump kept a constant tap-tap-tapping on the foyer floor, and the sound of her deep rose-hued taffeta dress with the slightly flounced skirt rustled slightly as she paced. At 6:40, Jill pulled up in front and Cathy slipped into her blue wool coat and dashed to the car.

The trip out the highway and to the base was a short one, and they were soon pulling up to the gate. Telling the impassive guard, "'B' Company NCO club, Sergeant Harmon," he passed them through with only a glance and wave of his hand. Then, "to the stop sign, turn right, go three streets and turn left one block."

According to the directions Joe had given her it was on the corner. They found it easily, parked the car in the designated space for visitors and walked toward the unadorned building. It was an A-frame with a low-pitched sloping gray roof and white painted boards girdling it. With only a few windows, it was a look-alike of almost every building on base, except this one featured a raised deck with eight steps leading up to the door.

They took the steps, and, inhaling a deep breath, Cathy reached for the short horizontal handle on the door. She never made contact as two soldiers, laughing and yelling to each other, slammed their way out pushing the handle away from her hand. The door hit her shoulder glancingly, but unbalanced her enough to force her against the railing surrounding the deck.

Apologizing profusely and helping her to right herself, the two men kept insisting on buying the ladies a drink inside in an attempt to make amends.

Getting herself squared away and finding she was totally unhurt, Cathy politely declined the offer. "I'm fine, fellas. Really. I'm meeting Sergeant Harmon. Is he here yet?"

"No, Miss, not yet," they replied.

The men, completely apologetic and further reassured she was all right, look at each other and without another word went on down the steps and on their way.

Stepping into the room was like a smoke bomb had been released, the haze so thick it felt as if it needed to be sliced in strips to get through.

An L-shaped long bar paralleled the right wall with the short end of the "L" to the center of the room; card and pool tables surrounded a tiny ten or twelve foot square wooden dance floor in the middle of the room. There were a few soldiers playing billiards, some were playing cards or dominoes, but most were talking and drinking, or listening to a jukebox siren dishing out a very mournful love song.

Moving to the bar, the girl's shimmied up onto tall stools, and the bartender ambled over to take their order.

Looking around and not seeing Joe, Cathy asked, as she slipped the black gloves off her fingers, "Sergeant Joe Harmon hasn't been in yet, has he?"

Corporal Jeremiah Griswold wasn't one who held back. This bar has been his job for a long time now, and he was proud that he knew most of the men's names.

Reaching across the bar, he held out a soft pudgy hand with short fingers, gave a quick shake to Cathy, then Jill's hand and said, "Nope, not here yet, Miss, but soon will be, I'm sure. Never misses at least a short time 'most every night of the week. Does he know you're coming?"

"Yes," replied Cathy. "He invited us."

With that knowledge, Corporal Griswold, or 'Griz' as he told them he preferred to be called, nodded and then fixed their requests of Manhattans and set each before them.

The girls started reaching into their purses to get money out, and 'Griz' shook his head and declined it. "Your moneys' no good in here, ladies. Besides, Harmon would have my hide if I allowed a lady friend of his to pay for a drink."

Jill, and a man who was sitting at a table alone listening to the jukebox, caught each other's eye. She smiled at him and whispered to Cathy, "I don't care if he's not an officer, he is so good looking, don't you agree? I can't wait forever for an officer to come along, now can…," she stopped. "Oh, good, he's coming over."

A couple of other soldier's in fatigue uniforms sidled up beside the girls and started a conversation with them.

"Where ya from? Where do you live?" and, "Why haven't we seen you here before?" was about all the further they got, when 'Griz' casually mentioned, "The ladies are here to meet Sergeant Harmon. Do you want to buy their drinks while they're waiting?"

A couple of them shelled out for the drinks, then excused themselves and scattered back along the bar and returned to whatever conversations they had been having.

"I'm sure he'll be along any minute now," 'Griz' encouraged Cathy.

Another drink down, and it was soon going to be eight o'clock, and Cathy was worrying that maybe she had somehow misunderstood Joe. Maybe he hadn't meant tonight. But surely, she couldn't have misunderstood him, could she?

It was eight-twenty when the phone rang. 'Griz' listened for a moment, glancing quickly up at the girls grunting a low "affirmative." He then listened for a bit longer, hung up the phone, and grabbing a towel and a glass began to rub a shine onto an already bright piece of stemware.

Stepping towards where the ladies were seated, he extended the apologies of Sergeant Harmon. "He's been ordered out on maneuvers, and won't make it to the club. He's sorry he couldn't have let you know sooner."

That said, 'Griz' took a deep breath, turned, and began polishing every glass he could find, stopping only when one of his patrons wanted another drink.

"Well, come on, Jill," Cathy grumbled. "We might as well go on home. Are you ready?"

Jill had found that the good-looking one was well on the verge of being a drunk one, and had also confided he was married. Sighing her great disappointment she agreed with Cath. "Sure, might as well," she pouted.

Cathy was furious, and not knowing the ways of the army yet didn't help at all. She was hurt, angry, disappointed, and worried. Was this something Joe did all the time? She didn't know.

"I wish I knew why he invited me there if he knew he was going on maneuvers, whatever that is," she fumed, as she slammed a door shut.

Each day she considered calling the number he had given her, but she wasn't brave enough.

There was nothing she could do but go on with her life, grudgingly go to work, then home at the end of her shift. And the thought kept popping into her head, suppose he's been just playing me along, and hadn't really wanted me to come after all?

She didn't expect him to call, but when he did, about two and one-half weeks later, she was very curt and irritated, and had an attitude of, "I could care less about talking with you."

"Why did you invite me there if you weren't going to be there," she finally threw at him angrily.

"Sorry, Cathy. They ordered me out so quickly I couldn't get to a phone to let you know. I am sorry and would like a chance to make it up to you. Please?"

He sounded so sincere she couldn't refuse his plea. Or, did she really want to? Since hearing his voice she couldn't deny now she wanted to see him again.

And his reason sounded, well, reasonable, to her. They talked a short while and he, apologizing again, soothed Cathy's feeling. The decision was made to go out again the coming Sunday.

When he picked her up that Sunday afternoon, Joe asked, "Have you been to the Garden of the Gods yet, Cathy?"

"No, but I've heard a lot about it. I'm told it's a beautiful place," she coolly countered.

"Well, I thought we might take a drive through there. It's cold today but most of it is in the car driving-through looking anyway."

With this goal in mind, they set out driving along the scenic highway leading to the beautifully shaped, red-colored rock that was fast becoming a tourist attraction of the world.

"This time of year there won't be too many people there, I'm sure," Joe stated. "So we should have it pretty much to ourselves."

And certainly his prediction was true. The area was pretty much deserted with only one car bearing a California license plate being there. He drove her through the trail of graveled road that led them around the most scenic views of the rocks.

And her almost constant, "Oh, my," and, "My goodness, that's so very beautiful," was very satisfying to Joe. He'd only been here once before, a long time ago, but seeing it now with the enthusiasm of Cathy's eyes was as if he were seeing it for the first time, and in some ways, he was. Cathy was picking out the quirky shapes, colors, contours and unusual placements of the different rocks to one another that he had not noticed when he was here the first time.

They finally stopped at an overview lot to see the area from above, and getting out of the car they walked to the railing and fence that lined the edge of the cliff.

"Wish I had brought my camera now," Cathy sighed regretfully. "I'd love to have some photo's of this."

"Well, now," Joe replied in a low throaty voice, looking at her, "We'll just have to do this place again in the near future, won't we, and we'll be sure you have your camera along then."

They were both leaning slightly over the railing, and as he was smilingly looking at her on his right, she was enthusiastically turning to her left to point, "Oh, look, over there, that tall one looks like the king of the place, doesn't it?"

She limply dropped her right arm when their faces came very close together and their eyes connected. Joe's smile disappeared, his face suddenly went so still. Only his eyes changed, very dramatically and quickly to a very dark hue. He looked at her mouth and then into her eyes with such soft yearning she could not pull away. With only the barest whisper of movement of his head, he leaned forward and kissed her, gently, on the lips.

When he pulled slightly back, Cathy's breath was taken away. He was so magnetic to her, her hands grabbed tightly onto the railing in an effort to keep from falling—or to keep from flinging herself into his arms, which was it she didn't know.

She only knew his lips burned into her like a branding iron, and she had never known such gentleness from a man. Backing away, stunned, beginning to breathe heavy, she turned herself from him for a moment to hide her confusion of feelings.

I don't know this man well enough to be feeling this way,she reproved herself silently. He's already stood me up once, so how do I know it won't happen again and again. He won't tell me what those 'maneuvers' are, so how do I know it's not…something else? 'Just army stuff' isn't much of an answer.

He wouldn't let her hide though. As these wild feelings whipped through her, she felt the world tilt as Joe turned her to face him, and, pulling her close to him by her shoulders he slowly enveloped her, gently pulling her against the hard wall of his chest.

He tilted her face up with his right hand, and their eyes locked like the popping of a key, and that key then thrown into a void. Looking at her with urgent tenderness, a blaze began to dance in his darkened eyes. His other arm came down and wrapped around her, imprisoning her very lightly against him, feeling her touch along the length of him.

Longing erupted inside her. She was mesmerized, beyond the point where she could object, and his hungering, searching mouth came down onto her full supple lips. She unhesitatingly let herself be explored, and explored, feeling the fast beat of his heart against her breast. His lips were like fire and ice, starting very sensitively, quickly becoming more urgent, more intense, very fierce and electrifying. His tongue parted her compliant lips, and slipped into the hollow of her mouth, searched briefly, then as quickly left her lips to scatter kisses over her upturned face, eyes, and hollow of her throat.

He lifted his head, and cradled Cathy's head on his shoulder. Strong, gentle arms pulled her closer and more intimate, curving her tightly against his own commanding body.

He buried his face in her silken hair, touched his lips to her forehead, enveloped her sweetness as close to himself as he could.

His kiss told her that he had been longing for someone who could touch him as no other could. She knew she was an exciting, precious woman to him by the way he held her so intimately and tenderly. She knew it without question. In aching amazement she knew she was the one who could liberate him of his long-ing. And her own, if he would only let her.

Her arms had had no choice but to glide their way around him, her fingers caressing the rippling muscles of his back, touching the smooth skin on his neck. She hung on for dear life, tightening her arms to pull him closer also. She was quivering now. She did not feel cold, but white-hot with the heat of his close-ness and she was ignited, her lips seeking the heated surface of his skin.

She kissed his cheeks, his throat, coming back to his willing mouth. She could feel tremors racing through his muscular frame as he searched, touched, explored her face and mouth, raining kiss after molten kiss upon her.

With a loud moan, he yanked his lips away, shuddering and shivering, feel-ing her body shake and tremble."Cathy," his voice husky and low. "Oh, Cathy."

They stood for what seemed centuries, or seconds; to each time had no meaning. They were monument still, holding each other very close. Not daring to move, both breathed deeply of each other, inhaling into each nostril the sub-stance of each other's scent, sensing every nerve and fiber of their bodies alive and tingling, and reveling in the heat that has stirred within them.

"Oh, yes, we'll come back to this Garden often," Joe was hoarsely whisper-ing in her ear. "I didn't know there were so many beautiful colors in these rocks. And listen, Princess, listen."

Cathy could hear nothing but the wind shuffling some leaves on the empty lot, the muted sound of an airplane soaring by in the distance, and the hammer-ing of her heart which she felt was bursting in her chest. Quiet. Pulsating. Vibrating-off-the-rocks sounds that brought even the smallest of resonations into sublime focus. She could also feel Joe's heart beating the same strong thumping music. Outwardly, it was very peaceful and calm, and gloriously colorful at the same time.

"That's what I mean, Princess, the quiet. You just don't find that easily anymore."

Joe was talking in a hushed voice, seemingly afraid of breaking the spell.

Solid, soft, hesitant voice; the feel of his breath against her ear sending tingles down her spine.

They lingered there for a short while until the wind started to throw a cold blanket of scattered snowflakes down upon them. Taking one last glance at the scene spread below them, and one more quick glance at each other, they hurried back to the car. Laughing giddily they fell into it breathlessly.

He had the motor running again and the welcome heat from the heater soon started to curl up on Cathy's legs. She stretched them out toward it, rubbing them briskly to warm them.

"Can I help you with that?" teased Joe.

"No, thank you. I can manage just fine," she retorted, beginning to blush. Chuckling softly, he pulled the car out of the lot, and inquired of her, "Princess, where would you like to go for something to eat? Are you hungry?"

"Famished," she smiled to him.

She discovered this to be true, her stomach not having had much of anything all day. She had been so nervous about seeing Joe again she could not eat earlier.

On the corner of Grant and Lafayette, they found, quite by accident, a cozy little Italian restaurant. The proprietor was a short, portly, and jovial man who took one look at them and surmised they would want, "the table back in the corner, all by yourselves, ah—no?" Agreeing with him, and glancing covertly at each other, they were led back to a table surrounded almost completely by large green planters and shrubbery hiding it from most of the rest of the dining room.

They noticed the dining room was small, yet each corner seemed to be decorated with just such a feeling of seclusion in mind. The red and white checkered tablecloth; the old wine bottle with colored candle wax dripping from it; and the small red-globed lamp on the edge of the table made it seem very romantic and that they were the only ones there.

A tall, slender, mustached waiter, sporting a long white wraparound apron, came to take their order and was very solicitous in explaining the menu to them. There was no written copy and he rolled off the litany of items to be had from memory, stopping now and again to see if there was anything catching his customers' fancy.

Leaving the spaghetti courses until last, he gave them the different types to be had.

When his recitation came to, "Thin pasta with marinara sauce and meatballs…", Cathy stopped him. "That's it for me. Also garden salad with the house dressing of 'poppy seed, honey, and red-wine vinegar', and iced tea, please."

Joe laid his hand across hers on the table. "That sounds fine to me also, but Bleu-cheese dressing on my salad, and cup of black coffee. But first," he smiled, "How about some wine to start off. Princess, what kind would you like?"

Having decided on a good red wine, the waiter left to get it and quickly returned with two chilled, beautiful, almost full glasses. They toasted each other with a clink, and the hot, crusty slices of bread he brought while they sipped were mouthwatering with sweet butter spread on them.

They could hardly wait for the salad to arrive and lunged into the cold, crisp lettuce and spinach immediately. There were vegetables sliced onto it, grated cheese spread on top, and the delicious dressing was sparingly poured over each one. They were delighted with each bite taken, and did not talk now. They looked into each others' eyes often, remembering their kiss.

Lingering a long while over the aromatic meal, it was all too soon for Cathy they decided to be on their way. The wind was drifting a light snow into shallow rows along the edges of the road and piling it up into small swirling heaps upon the uneven grasses and mounds of earth along their route to the car. Cathy marveled at its tenacity and beauty of motion, even as she wished for warm, balmy breezes so they could go for a walk.

Instead, they drove into the countryside and sat in the car at the end of a long twisting road that overlooked a shallow creek. They talked and cuddled, keeping at a decisive distance the repeating of the sensuous feelings that had exploded within them earlier. Joe still did not want to talk about his career life. He talked about everything else but that part of him, and Cathy felt nervous and edgy at his evasiveness. She wondered why he wouldn't talk about it, a touch of uneasiness striking her now and then throughout the evening.

Monday came and he was gone again, and she felt somewhat justified at her apprehension. This time he was gone almost three weeks, and she was about out of her mind with worry and anger the entire time.

Glenna came by the restaurant and told her Hank was gone also, so she couldn't contact him to find out anything about where Joe might be. But, she suspected, he wouldn't have told her anyway.

CHAPTER FOUR

She was reading a borrowed newspaper Sunday night when she spied an advertisement that caught her eye. Cathy had been thinking for a long time, off and on, about what she wanted as a career, knowing that being a waitress was not what she aspired to be the rest of her working life. She was also determined to go on living in the best way possible when Joe was gone.

The ad seemed to loom out to her with its bold letters that proclaimed: "You can be a legal secretary in three short months with higher wages and better working conditions that will improve your lifestyle." She read on about how easy it would be for, "Ambitious, talented, and deserving young women to enroll in classes that are to start in two short weeks. No money down. A typing test will determine if you qualify. For further information, call 555-5324."

She read and reread it, and the more she scanned it, the more determined she was to give it a try, more determined than ever not to be dependent on anyone, especially a soldier who deserted her without any explanations.

The very next morning she called the number, and was told to be at the agency at two o'clock the following Thursday afternoon. Immediately dragging out an old portable typewriter from the closet, she wound paper onto its roller and began a series of typing exercises that was remembered from school days.

Oh, damn! she groused, I haven't touched this thing for a long time. I've got to do well enough to pass the test and get out of that restaurant and better myself. It's getting to be too painful there anymore. Inexpert fingers and stiff keys did not make it easy to concentrate on hitting the right ones for the right place in her practice sentences.

Cathy spent the following day also practicing, and cursing those keys that wanted to stick and pile up at the least provocation of her fingers. But when she completed a paragraph that was almost error-free, she felt tremendous progress had been made in just two short days. Her fingers were now sore from the unaccustomed exercises but she continued to concentrate on the upcoming test, trying to keep her excitement about it, but images of Joe kept interrupting her thoughts.

Somewhat depressed, she went to work that Tuesday night, plodding through her routine chores with very little enthusiasm, wondering where Joe was, angry at, and missing him.

As she cleaned her stations before going off duty, she looked up just as a customer was sliding sideways into one of her booths, and with a start she realized, Joe's home.

Anger rushed forward and dominated the feelings within her and she turned away, stalking with a furious stride into the women's locker room.

Cathy kicked her foot against a locker. Dammit! Who does he think he is anyhow? Just waltz in here at one o'clock in the morning and expect me to be ready to wilt in his arms or something? Well, he can just go blow it out his ear. She paced the floor in fuming frustration.

After a few minutes, which allowed her to cool down a bit, she cracked the door a little and peered cautiously out. Why doesn't he just leave? I'm not coming out until he does. Have had it with his disappearance act. Gone for almost three weeks and just show up, not have the decency to call, or anything.

Maybe he'll get the message, get tired of waiting and just leave. He better realize I've had just about enough! She hid there for what seemed a long time.

As she furiously paced up and down the room, she began to think, On second thought, why should I fuss about this? Hmmph, I'm not obligated to him, and he certainly is not obligated to me. She took in a deep calming breath, put on a bravado face and walked out of the locker room expecting to see him there.

He wasn't. Looking toward the booth, she recognized, I really did want to see him after all, and then felt really despondent and more aggravated. Going to the exit she gave a halfhearted wave of goodnight to her fellow workers and went on out into the night.

She had gotten into the habit of walking home even at such a dangerous hour of the morning. It was three blocks of well-lit and mostly deserted streets, yet the vice-patrol police kept an eye on her, most nights escorting her the entire way home, talking to her from the window of their car. They were regular customers at the restaurant and knew who the 'pick-ups' were, and they knew she was not one of them. They protected her, and asked her to keep an eye out for runaway underage girls walking the streets not having a home to go to. She had seen many of these youth's run into alleyways to hide or even run to a passing car, having waved the young men down, and get in when they saw the police car coming down the street.

Approaching the walkway leading to her apartment, she waved her thanks to the police as they left her to drive back downtown.

When she walked up the steps and started to set her key into the lock, she heard a sound, and wheeling around found Joe standing on the steps she had just come up. Her breathing stopped.

"Please, Cathy, don't be scared. I'm sorry if I frightened you just now," Joe was saying fervently and softly.

Her heart started a familiar hammering. "Joe, what are you doing here? I thought you were gone when I didn't see you at the restaurant anymore. I'm not sure I want to…," his kiss covered her mouth before all the words were out. He had reached out, pulled her to him and was kissing her persuasively and sweetly, his hands caressing her back and shoulders as he drew her tighter. All Cathy could do, to keep from falling when her legs went wobbly, was hold onto him.

Yet resentment and frustration welled up stronger with each passing second.

Finally, he released her slightly and was instantly concerned when he saw the tears brimming in her eyes. "Oh, Princess, please don't. I'm sorry things are the way they are."

He held her, cradled her, tried to soothe her tears away, only making it worse on Cathy's emotions and the droplets came faster.

She whispered harshly, "Joe, what are you doing off base on a Tuesday? You told me you couldn't get away from the base on a weeknight. What's going on, and is Hank with you? Glenna has been to the restaurant several times, and she doesn't know where Hank is either. She's really upset, as I've been."

Cathy was trying to focus on something...anything, to keep from losing her balance of emotion any more than she already had.

"Yeh, Hank's back at base, and he'll call Glenna tomorrow morning. Everything's okay," Joe said softly. "Can we go inside and talk please? It's really kind of hard to whisper out here in the cold and not have the neighbors hear."

Cathy unlocked the door and held it open, inviting him in with a sweep of her hand.

"I'll put some coffee on," she sniffed as she walked blindly toward the kitchen wiping at her eyes. "Please, have a seat anywhere."

Instead, Joe followed her into the kitchen and, glancing at her for permission, took the aluminum percolator from her hand and filled it with water. Docilely she handed him the coffee can, and he filled the required amount into the upper chamber, then plugged it in at the outlet above the stove.

Cathy was glad now she had stopped at the bakery and picked up some very large chocolate chip cookies on the way to work yesterday. She had gotten most of them home by putting them in her locker at the restaurant where her co-workers couldn't get to them. She brought them out and laid them on a plate on the counter.

They weren't talking yet, and she retreated to the bathroom to repair her face.

When she left, Joe was intently watching the bubbles of the coffeepot sprouting and bubbling in the glass dome of the lid, and when it had quit its burbling and singing, he pulled the plug, opened the lid and removed the basket to empty the depleted grounds into the nearby wastebasket.

Cathy walked silently back into the kitchen, wordlessly reached into the cabinet to pull two coffee mugs from the shelf.

Joe poured the hot steaming coffee into them. Each took it black, and carrying the mugs into the living room both sat down on the small flowered couch, the cookies forgotten. She reached over and turned on the light of a small lamp on the table nestled between the couch and easy chair.

Cathy was very tense, as Joe appeared to be. They leaned against the soft material of the couch, sat quietly for a time, heard a clock strike the quarter hour, sipped their brew.

Upset, uneasy, burning her tongue on the hot coffee and not totally realizing it, or caring.

After a few moments, Joe turned his body and sat sideways, his back against the high full arm, and brought his knees halfway up onto the edge of the couch. He studied Cathy, looking at her over the brim of his coffee mug.

Trying desperately to get her jittery nerves under control, she searched madly in her thoughts for how to voice her frustrations. But it was Joe who broke the silence, haltingly, choosing his words carefully as he spoke in a low, emotion-laden voice.

"Cathy, I can't tell you anything about what I'm doing. I can only ask that you trust me, and believe me when I say that I've never felt as strongly about anyone in my life as I do about you." A deep breath, "There are going to be times when I'm going to be gone for very long stretches, and I won't be able to tell you I'm going, or when I'll be back. And yep, Hank's involved too. He can't tell Glenna anything either."

Cathy set her mug onto the coffee-table and glanced at him, an angst-ridden foreboding welling within her, and a prickly feeling starting on the back of her neck from the look of agitation on Joe's flushed face.

"Please, Princess," he continued, "I know too well that I should never have allowed... us... to happen. But I'm human, drawn to you so strongly I couldn't stop myself from getting to know you. Feelings such as we have are so rare and precious that I couldn't let my life go by without tasting them," his voice lowering to a dejected exhalation, "even if I live to regret it the rest of my life." He reached over and put his hand lightly on her arm.

"Joe, what you just said scares me horribly," Cathy quivered. "What do you mean?"

She withdrew her arm from his touch hesitantly. "Why should you have to regret knowing me? I don't understand that at all. Does all this have to do with those trips you take? Am I going to one day find you no longer around, and..." she gasped with a sudden, palling premonition, "I'll never know if you're alive or...?"

She couldn't say it. Shaking her head she inhaled deeply, her eyes wide with newfound fright from the look of despair on his face giving her the answer.

She whispered, "Is that it... you could be gone and not come back, and I'd never know what happened to you!" A feeling of panic was rising in her, a feeling of slowly being drowned.

Joe's eyes and brow were pinched and furrowed. He shook his head in a quick jerk of 'yes' with a lift of his shoulders, his gaze never leaving her face.

"From what I'm...imagining," Cathy continued sluggishly, "are you saying that what you're involved in is... dangerous... stuff?"

Springing up from the couch she paced the room as if a small whirlwind had caught up with her. "Joe, I don't know if I can handle this. Am I to understand that what's happened twice now since we've known each other can happen any time...for any length of time... not knowing... anything? Or, is there someone I can find out from, when... or if, you're coming back?" She was shaking in exasperation and bewilderment in her query. "No?"

He was moving his head in a slow negative answer.

She pleaded very softly through chattering teeth, "No, I don't think I can handle this. You'd better go for now, Joe. Please."

Without a word he put his coffee mug quietly down onto the coffee-table and stood up slowly. He reached his hands out to her, then dropped them in futility, and went to the door. With eyes full of pain, he looked back at her once from inside the door frame before closing the door quietly behind him.

Cathy's eyes were brimming with tears as his footsteps faded away down the sidewalk. She heard a car motor start down the street, then it hummed softly and was soon out of hearing completely in the still night.

That night she pounded her pillow in agitation, playing again and again in her mind every word that had gone between them, every nod of the head, blink of an eye. The circle of magnetism that surrounded her whenever she was near him still held her captive in her thoughts, and Cathy couldn't find sleep at all, tossing and turning, crying through the entire night.

She watched with red swollen eyes the dawn light rise in her window, and then arose and stumbled to the kitchen for a cup of coffee. The pot from the evening before still stood on the counter, nearly half full with the brew Joe had made, and seeing it started the tears anew. The smell of it was still there. As she had walked into the kitchen the image of him standing there hunched over the cabinet watching the coffee bubble and sputter will always be with her. Taunting her. Mocking her. Tearing her apart.

Fitfully, she drained it into the sink and started with fresh water and coffee, and sat watching it percolate and sing much as Joe had, but by then her stomach was too tied up in knots, and she couldn't drink it. Sighing, she took a jar of juice from the fridge and poured the golden liquid into the mug she had gotten out for her coffee.

Her mind settled. She had to see Joe again and talk it out with him as best they could. She went to the phone, "Jill, can I borrow your car tonight, please? I have to go to the NCO to see Joe. No, I need to go alone this time, hon. Would you pick me up, then I'll take you back since it's only a few blocks? It's really very important, Jill."

She next called the manager at the restaurant and asked for the night off. Having done both, she lay down again and slept, restlessly.

At two o'clock in the afternoon, she had had enough, and stepped into a hot shower under the needle spray for a long and refreshing shampoo and bath, hoping to revitalize herself.

Feeling physically enormously better, she dressed carefully, deciding to go out for something to eat, then head for the base at six-thirty. She also decided not to call and let Joe know she was coming; she brooded about whether he was going to welcome her.

Will he want to see me again? Maybe he would think it best if we called it quits now; I obviously can't be a part of all of his life. What will he say about my just showing up; will he even be there?

Cathy might not have worried so much if she had known he would welcome her so warmly. He'd arrived at the NCO just a few minutes before her, still in his fatigue uniform of the day.

When he saw her come in, he went to her immediately, and, with a warm welcoming smile and only a brief, "Hi, Princess", put his arm around her waist and ushered her back out the door. He started walking down the gravel path toward the parade ground, smiling and looking at her with blue eyes sparkling a warmth that said he was glad she had come, but did not say a word.

It was getting dark and as soon as they were out of sight of the buildings he swung her to him and kissed her lightly, lingering and savoring the sweetness of her lips.

"I'm glad you came tonight, Princess, but I thought you had to work," he breathed to her. He was holding her carefully and slightly away from him, and it was all Cathy could do to control herself and not embrace him tightly, forgetting everything else.

Tears were on the brink of falling.

"I had to see you, Joe. I took the night off because I couldn't leave things the way they were last night." Cathy's lips were trembling, and putting her hands up, she cradled his face, speaking earnestly and without hesitation.

"Even though I'm still afraid because of what you told me, I believe, too, that what we have is worth some... bad times... of my not knowing where you are or if you're all right. I tried, all night long, God knows, imagining not having any time at all with you, and it doesn't work, doesn't feel right," her voice a husky low murmur, "and I don't know what else to do, except to accept you for how you are," a shuddering sigh, "and for how it is."

Cathy was visibly shaking, and he enveloped her in the velvet steel of his arms, held her, swayed with her, both of them trembling, softly whispering to her, kissing her hair, her face.

"It's all right, sweet Princess, it's all right." Tears also shimmered in his eyes.

They walked again, and, coming to the deserted bleachers at the parade ground, they sat down on the bottom plank. Joe, straddling the seat, again pulled Cathy close to him with her shoulder tight against his chest. The wind was mild tonight with only a light stinging feel, and neither one noticed it that much.

Joe seemed elated to see Cathy, and she burrowed her head into his shoulder, holding him close. He began talking to her in a rasping and tenuous voice, clearing his throat, "We really need to discuss some things you need to know, Cathy, and I can't think of a better time then now. Is that all right? I mean, now?"

From his tone, she began to lightly bite at her lower lip in some anxiety, but nodded her head agreeably.

"Do you remember, when I told you about Hank, Mike, and myself being in Korea? Well, we were there some of the time... in..." rasping out the last word, "...hell!"

At Cathy's startled inhalation of breath he continued.

"We were in a fighting 'confrontation' as the powers that be liked to call it, and we lost a particular hill for awhile—sweetie, it really doesn't matter which one—but we lost it long enough for our company to be overrun," he hesitated briefly drawing in his breath, "and we were taken."

"Taken?" Cathy exclaimed, very puzzled. "What do you mean by 'taken'?"

"We were taken prisoners-of-war, Princess," he returned bitterly, "on the Fourth of July. July Fourth holidays aren't, for me anyway, like what they used to be when I was a kid; I used to love the fireworks and sparklers." Soft, vehemently voiced curses escaped from his lips which were pressed tightly into Cathy's hair.

Holding her close they sat for a long, apprehensive pause.

Then with a deep sigh, he hesitantly began to talk again.

"I haven't told you this, Princess, but I was engaged to be married before I went to Korea, to a girl from 'Philly', Therese Anne. It was one of those relationships that we grew up in, dated all through high school, and our parents had us all set up, in their minds, for housekeeping before we were even out of school. But I promised her we would be married when I got back from Korea." He asked, "I think I told you I joined the army right from high school?" Cathy acknowledged his question with an abrupt nod.

"Anyway, they did things to us in that prison camp, Cathy. When we were freed at the end of the war, I wrote Therese about… well, just some of the things that happened, my intention being of not wanting to shock her all at once, especially about how my physical appearance had changed. I believed I could tell her anything, that she was my best friend."

His gaze went far away, far away from the army compound, from her, and beyond where anyone else could see. His voice choked to a hoarse whisper. "We all looked pretty bad coming out of there, skin and bones thin, hair about all gone—well, mine, anyway, since never had much since teenager—and scars all over our body's. Cathy…," he shuddered and dropped his forehead on her shoulder briefly, then lifted it and continued, "I have one-hundred twenty-seven scars from cigars and cigarettes they put out on my skin." His breathing was in heavy grunting spasms. "Mike and Hank were there, too."

He took several deep wavering breaths. "But we didn't sweat that small stuff. It was when they took my… manhood… I…." His voice faltered and stopped. Then, hissing through his teeth, jaw clamped tight, "I had to let Therese know we could never have children of our own. She's a typical Catholic big-family girl, and I wasn't brave enough to tell her face to face. I wrote her about being…," he gasped a sharp intake of breath, "… what happened. It was part of the therapy we had to go through at the hospital." His face, now turned to the sky, was etched in agony in the slowly rising pale moonlight, his utterances so low that Cathy could only close her eyes tightly, listen, and hold him.

Slowly, haltingly, he continued, "Princess, we all spent several weeks in the hospital in Japan before they would let us come back to the States, and Therese was there waiting for me at the dock when I came home, or so my parents told me later. She took one look at me and she ran, not to me, but away from me. I never even saw her in the crowd. I was still fifty-five pounds down from when I left and she knew that. I guess everything just scared her too much. She wouldn't see me, and anyway," again a deep shattering sigh, "two weeks later, her brother phoned me and said she'd run off and married some salesman she'd just met."

Joe's voice seemed tired, dejected, as if he had relived it all again in those last few moments.

"Her family was about as sick about the whole mess as I was. I'd bought her a beautiful, two-carat diamond ring in Japan with some of the accumulated monies of my back pay. She never knew that, and when she was gone, there was no reason for me to keep it anymore. So I walked...," a deep breath, and dejectedly, "so I walked onto the bridge over the Delaware river... and... and... tossed it... to the fish. I... almost...followed it... over the rail."

Cathy had not interrupted him at any point of his discourse. But when he stopped, his eyes were wet, and he raggedly and coarsely swore almost inaudibly under his breath, his face still lifted to the sky. She wrapped her arms around his chest, the tears flowing freely down her face against his shoulder. Totally speechless, she didn't know how to comfort him, or if there was a way to comfort him.

"Princess," he continued, "that's why I do what I do now. I signed right after Therese Anne for a section of the service called G2, and it has evolved rapidly to other titles, most of it involving Army Intelligence work. And...," he stopped, "and...," ever so cautiously, "I have many reasons to do what I can, against those bastards who did what they did, to all of us in that camp... and others. You have to swear not to repeat this to anyone, Cathy, because it could mean my life. I mean about what I'm doing now. But then, if there was the slightest hint that I didn't believe I could trust you, you wouldn't be hearing it."

Urgently now, "I'm telling you because I want you to understand why I'm gone when I am. I will never, I repeat never, tell you anything what I'm actually doing, or where I've been, and you will never ask, and I am unshakable about that." Even in the nippy breeze, tiny beads of sweat covered his face and forehead from his efforts. Cathy was stunned, distressed, about what he and these men must have suffered through. She couldn't even imagine what the 'many reasons' could be, and she didn't really want to think about it. All she knew was that she wanted to hold Joe and kiss him and take away some of the pain of his memories.

Suddenly she understood, somewhat, his gentleness. He evidently had known so much brutality, torture, and cruelty, he could not bring himself to be harsh or mean, knowing firsthand what it could do to the human spirit and mind; anyway, not with her he couldn't. If he had another side to his nature in his work, she didn't want to know at this time. She'd witnessed his self-control with Terry at the Gringo Bar; his walking away instead of confrontation with her last night. Was that the real inner man?

His path was chosen a long time before Cathy met him, and she now understood that she had to accept what he could give when their paths did cross. Her mind was very shaken by the revelations he had told her; her heart felt heavy with sadness.

Cathy had asked no questions, there was no discussion. He had laid out his life history, and future, before her, and she had to accept it as it was. To her that was enough for now.

She pulled his face down to her and caressed with her lips his cheeks, his mouth, moving to under his chin and onto his neck where his collar stood open at the top. She brought his hand to her lips and lightly pressed kisses in the palm.

He moaned softly and gathered her against him again, his tremulous seeking mouth claiming hers. Moving her to be able to bring the hand she had just kissed under her coat and pullover sweater, he reached under her blouse and pushed up her bra revealing the softness of her bare breasts, then caressed them with exquisite tenderness, lightly feeling and fondling them, exploring, touching, his thumb gently circling the taut buds.

Drawing herself up to allow his exploration, she melted into the ecstasy he was creating within her; the fire his touch was lighting was becoming almost unbearable. She was thrillingly aware of him now also, his manliness tight against her thigh.

Suddenly, he stopped. "Princess, this can't happen. Not here, not now." His voice was a faltering whisper, his breathing quick and shuddering.

They were both shivering, and his passion quickly transferred to arms that wrapped covetously round her. He held her so tight that breathing could have been a problem, if she weren't breathing so hard, and her racing heart surely must be keeping blood circulation from being cut off. They sat a long time in the rapture of feeling each other so close, but the intense recalling of the words spoken just a few minutes before could not be erased from Cathy's mind.

After some time, calmer now, yet her voice quavering, still trying to push aside the need she was feeling, she quietly told him, "Joe, I'm taking a typing test tomorrow afternoon. I'm trying to get into secretarial school to get a better job."

"Hey, that's great, Princess." He smiled, his voice still tremulous. "With a day job, maybe we'd be able to see each other more often through the week. Good luck, sweetie." He planted kisses on her fingers, than slowly stood up and restlessly glanced skyward.

"We'd better head back. The moon isn't going to get very bright, and I think it'll get pretty dark out here. The M.P.'s might mistake us for sneakers and give us some trouble. Come on, Princess, we better go." Helping her up they stood holding onto each other. He kissed her face, neck, her lips, pulling her flush against himself, crushing her hips and breasts into his own pulsing body.

Nuzzling his mouth near her ear, he whispered, "You're the best person that has happened to me in my life in an awfully long time, Princess."

Strolling on the gravel path toward the car, side by side with their arms locked around each other's waist was hard for Cathy. She wanted to be with him longer tonight, but it was getting too late and she was going to have to leave. He told her civilians had to be off the base by 9 p.m.

CHAPTER FIVE

Thursday morning was overcast, rainy, and a dreary beginning of a day for Cathy, but she didn't mind it too much. Remembering the evening before was a mixture of emotions. Her nerves were still tense, and sadness for Joe's many revelations to her were uppermost in her mind, but the taste of his amorous advances were very delicious to her heart.

The typing test was scheduled for two p.m., and she decided to put in a couple hours of practice before going to the agency where the test was being held. Forcing herself to concentrate, she pushed paper after paper through the roller of the typewriter, sometimes cursing the keys as they tended to be sticky from years of non-use, and her fingers not yet trained to hit the right ones.

Finally, with a sigh, she put the typewriter away, and went to her bedroom to get ready to leave. On a day like today she wished she had her own car, but her finances being as they were, knew she couldn't even come close to affording one. She helped Jill with gas and maintenance costs on her car when she could, and Jill loaned the use of the car when she could. Jill had inherited the car from her father who had passed away a year earlier, or she probably wouldn't have one either; the mutual help they gave was a satisfying one, as they liked and respected each other.

But today was going to have to be a bus day. Carrying her blue and white striped umbrella, and wearing a simple cream woolen skirt, white blouse and blue suit jacket, she slipped her galoshes on over her black pumps and started out for the bus stop two blocks away. She only had one transfer to deal with on the bus route, and she had started early enough to allow plenty of time. Thank heaven the buses ran on a fairly accurate schedule.

Arriving at the center, she walked into the marble-front building and had an immediate feeling of misgiving as most of the ladies who were waiting in the foyer were intimidating in their fresh professional appearance. Having spent all her working life in uniforms of one sort or another, she had not needed to improve her wardrobe for the business world, and now felt very inadequate in her year-old skirt and two-year-old jacket.

Finding a seat, after registering her name at the desk, she took the opportunity to look around, but had only a short few minutes. The efficient receptionist almost immediately announced they were ready to escort the ladies to the exam room, and, "Would you all follow me please?" brought everyone to their feet.

The applicants were told to start at the front row and align themselves at a typewriter as they entered the room.

Finding herself in the third row, at the third typewriter, she examined the machine. It was a very elite model, much more sophisticated then what she had worked on, and comparing it to her own was, well, no comparison.

The manager was giving instructions on how the test was to be completed, and she inquired as to whether everyone was familiar with these machines. Several hands went up, including Cathy's, giving notice of need for a little instructional assistance. The personnel were very accommodating to the six or seven who needed help, and Cathy's confidence took a little leap for the better.

But the test itself was a nightmare for her. Accuracy in timed sequences, and speed, was what they were looking for and the few days' worth of practice she had had was not enough for her to compete. She knew when she left the room at the end of that hour that she was not going to be going to this school, and somewhat dejectedly headed for home.

Arriving there thirty minutes later, Cathy changed into her uniform and headed out for the restaurant. Her mood was very low and all the, "Well, you could try later when they offer this class again and you have had some more practice," coming from her co-workers didn't help too much.

What really helped was Joe's telephone call about 7:30 that evening. Just hearing his voice helped, and his consideration of her in the telling of the days' catastrophic test cheered her tremendously. He teased her, cajoled her, told her it wasn't the end of the world, and, "Don't sweat the small stuff, Princess," brought her around immediately. She laughed with him then at the recalling of how, "my fingers refused to obey any command on those damnable keys, and," she surmised, "I guess it just isn't the right time for me for this particular switch in my life."

A brief pause, "Am I going to see you this weekend, Joe?"

"I'm planning on it, and looking forward to it. Sunday afternoon?"

"Yes, if it's a nice day maybe we can pack a picnic lunch and go back to the 'Garden'. Would you like that?"

"Oh, yeah!" he sighed, "I'd like that a lot."

The rest of that night and the next two nights of work were a blur to her; time passed so slowly when one was wanting a time in the future to hurry and appear.

Sunday finally did arrive. Joe called about noon and stated he had been worried because she didn't answer when he had tried calling earlier.

She laughed, "Well, I was at ten a.m. Mass at St. Joseph's. I didn't know you were going to call, or I would have gone earlier so I wouldn't miss you."

"You're Catholic?" Joe had an astonished sound in his voice.

"Yes, I guess the subject never came up, did it?"

"No, it didn't. I am, too. Catholic, I mean."

The icing on her cake. Cathy couldn't have had any better news in her life than this. Joe was Catholic also! It wouldn't have mattered, it didn't matter, but it was the icing on her beautiful cake.

"What time can you make it, Joe? I have the lunch about ready. It's such a pretty day I don't want to waste a minute of it. You don't think it'll be too cold for a picnic, do you?"

"I'll be there in about twenty minutes, and we can be on our way. Is that time enough? And if it's too cool, we'll eat in the car."

"I'll be ready."

When he knocked on her door, Cathy's heart leaped, and when she opened it and was swooped into his arms so quickly and eagerly, she knew this was going to be a glorious day with him.

She pulled herself away and commanded him to, "Please, pick up the picnic basket and we'd better go, or we'll never get out of this apartment if you keep this up." Her cheeks were a charming blush of pink, and a colossal smile lit up her face and eyes.

He laughed with delight, nuzzled her nose with his, then obediently walked over to the chair she had placed the basket on, and picked it up. When she had locked the door, he took her arm with his free one and led her towards the dark blue Chevy.

They spent the afternoon touring the beautiful rock gardens again, joking and flirting with each other. They had partaken of the fried chicken, potato salad, fresh tomato slices, and fresh fruit with cheese Cathy had packed, on a blanket they laid out in one of the areas of the park set apart for picnicking. Joe had brought a delicious white wine to round out the feast.

She had remembered the camera this time, and they made many pictures of the magnificent rock formations and shapes. The sun was asserting itself and showing its bright face for them, casting interesting and elongated shadows behind and surrounding some rocks; these shadows giving an even more intangible mystery and majesty to them.

They drove into 'their' spot at the overview lot and captured many more views of the panorama below, some with Joe in the foreground, and he took some of her, demanding, "I want some of those pictures when they're developed, Princess."

"We'll see, Joe," she demurely teased. "I'm not very photogenic and we'll see how they turn out first."

They watched the sun set behind the rocks, making photos of the constantly changing rose, lavender, purple and bright orange streaks of color cast upon the low hanging clouds. Cathy always had loved watching a sun set, but tonight was special, and she hoped it was special to Joe, too.

Hugging her with her back against his chest, "I've always liked watching sunsets, Cathy, maybe about as much as a sunrise. A sunrise is somewhat fresher in color, more pure maybe. Sunsets tend, in my humble estimation, to have the days' dirt hanging in the atmosphere. It gives beautiful colors too, but not as clean-looking somehow."

Cathy thought maybe Joe had been reading her mind again, and said as much.

"Well, I haven't seen a lot of sunrises. I usually work late, then sleep late, but I know I love beautiful sunsets. I'm going to have to make an effort to watch some morning, and compare them myself." Looking up at him with a smile,

"I'm glad you like them, too."

She could get very sentimental about a radiant sunset. The gorgeous range of hues and blends of aristocratic color always brought shivers to her soul in it's display.

"I firmly believe the Artist of this palette is giving us the least of what He can show so as to not burn our hearts out."

It gave her the 'goose bumps' if she thought too much about it.

And then, too soon, it was gone. The glow of oranges and reds left streaks on the horizon and faded ever so slowly into a deep purple and disappeared.

They had gone, before completion of sundown, to the car to sit and watch as the wind had become a lot cooler. They snuggled with Joe lying on the front seat half-lazing across Cathy's lap, his shoulder resting against her door, the blanket rolled up behind his back as a cushion.

Sitting this way, intermittently kissing and talking, wiled away time. It wasn't until the Park Ranger came by stabbing the light of his flashlight into the car they realized time had gotten away from them, and the park was closing for the night. Apologizing to the Ranger, Joe sat up and started the car engine, put it into gear and drove slowly out of the overview lot and onto the road leading to the highway.

It was after getting through the gate and out of the park boundaries they looked at each other and burst into hilarious laughter, laughing until tears ran and Joe could hardly see to drive. He pulled into an open lot along the road and stopped the car.

Laughter, the release that was sorely needed, in part, to fling away the emotional stress they were remembering from their first visit to the top of the hill.

"Man, it's been one helluva long time since I've been 'lighted' by a policeman for parking!" he laughed, wiping his eyes with a handkerchief. Cathy was doubled over yet as she laughed. "I can't recall ever being, what did you call it, 'lighted'? But it's funny. That poor ranger must have thought, what, heavens, who knows?"

They soon gained control of themselves again and Joe proceeded down the road, a snicker emanating now and again from both of them.

Joe asked her softly, "Where are we going, Princess? I don't really feel like doing any barhopping tonight. Where do you suggest, a late movie?"

"I'm hungry. That lunch was a long time ago. What say we go for something to eat, then decide about a late movie or not."

"That's fine." Joe was eyeing her mischievously out the corner of his eyes, "I don't have to be back on base until six in the morning, or just in time to go to work."

Cathy understood, all right, what he was suggesting, and she shivered inside her body at the thought. But no, that was going too fast for her, and she tried to ignore his implication.

"I believe after we eat, we had better find a late movie to go to," she replied in a somber voice.

"Oh? Have you decided that's what you want to do?" he asked in a roguish manner.

"No," she countered softly, "not what I want to do, but what we are going to do."

He chuckled at her then, reached out his arm and drew her up against his side, hugging her.

"Are you sure?" he whispered.

"Very sure. Let's stop here at Bannons. They have a delicious hot roast beef and whipped potato plate that is out of this world. What say, can you settle for that, or would you like something else?"

As soon as the words were out of her mouth, Cathy knew they had come out in a way that Joe was going to take it out of context, and she blushed at his loud crack of laughter that followed.

"Yes, my precious, I'll settle, for hot roast beef and whipped potato for tonight," came through his mirthful chuckling.

They ended up going to an all night theater after their dinner. A double-feature, both of which were rousing swashbucklers with Errol Flynn as a pirate in each. The theater crowd hissed, booed, or cheered at each unfolding event, getting into the story as though it were a stage play with the characters hearing the responsive audience. They threw handfuls of popcorn at the screen. It was fun, different, and it was the wee hours of the morning when it was let out.

Walking Cathy to her door, he stopped under the overhang, raised an eyebrow above those blue lagoons, hinting for her to invite him in. Very, very sleepy now, Cathy answered that question by rising up on her tiptoes and kissing him a quiet and sweet goodnight.

He quickened his hold on her and brought her tight against himself, breathing deeply. "I'll call you tomorrow, Princess. Have sweet dreams."

He unlocked the door for her and stepped aside as she brushed against him and went in. He set the now empty picnic basket on the foyer floor, turned, and went back to the idling Chevy. Cathy heard the motor rev up and then pull the car slowly away from the curb and down the street.

Hmmm... he knew he wasn't staying tonight; why else would he leave the car idling? He is so sweet. She laid across the bed, pulled the quilt over her, and was sound asleep in seconds.

The next few weeks were rapturous one's for Cathy. The time she spent with Joe, and sometimes Hank and Glenna were with them, was busy and full of fun. They had many picnics in some of the beautiful scenic spots found in this part of the country.

Bicycling, walking hand in hand through the many parks and around the lakes that dotted the area were some of their favorite things to do; kissing under the canopy of trees, or racing each other around the edge of a tiny pond in a meadow on the mountain on one of their many horseback rides.

A trip to the top of Pike's Peak Mountain on a beautiful Sunday was the epitome of their fun time. It was a clear and majestic robin egg blue of a sun-filled day with only a few fleecy white clouds brightening the sky when they decided to go.

The four hired a limousine tour-car with a driver who knew the road and its hazards; this way they could enjoy the scenery without having to worry about watching where they were driving.

And what awesome scenery it was! The lofty peaks and sloping valleys that spread before them undulated and curved to meet each other coming and going. They were breathtaking, with patches of bluebells, yellow rose and lavender mountain columbine, flaming paintbrush, wild daisies, and many other early Spring multicolored wildflowers spreading their colors across the view. The trees, huge boulders, and sometimes a fox, rabbit, deer, and wild animals they saw excited their visual perception of what the mountain was made of. Some almost hidden patches of snow still clung in the deep crevices and holes.

The higher they went, the more rare the air was becoming, and the girls giggled at the light-headed feeling that assailed them.

"Nah, we're not feeling it," Joe and Hank both denied.

"You girls just aren't used to this kind of rare air." The more they denied it, the more Glenna and Cathy were convinced it affected the guys also, but no amount of joshing or teasing would get them to admit otherwise.

They spent an hour or so at the magnificent peak, following around the rail along the rim area, staring at all the views, making many photographs, and loitered awhile in the souvenir shop looking for just the right object to capture the memory of this adventure. A drink of hot chocolate and a freshly made doughnut at the Summit restaurant warmed their insides and helped to stamp off the chill air. Reluctantly, it was time to start down again. Finding their tour guide at the information center, they headed for the limousine and, laughing happily, tumbled into their seats, and he immediately had them on the sloping road down.

This drive down the steep, curving road was almost as awe-inspiring as the ride up; only this time the depth of the drop-offs seemed to be more evident because of the angle at which they were being viewed; the valleys and peaks seemed to be more extreme than before.

The sun was at a lower angle and cast a misty glow across the peaks as they rounded curve after curve, looking at it straight on, now from the left, then from the right, constantly changing and ever-fascinating.

The driver of the limousine, a very confident and almost cocky young man, loved telling stories of 'horror happenings' as he liked to put it; stories of private cars going up and overheating, forced to stop along the narrow curving road.

"Right here, folks, is where a private car coming down the road, a big Caddie I think, sideswiped a stopped car and bounced it enough the right wheels just dropped off the side, with two passengers still in the car. That was scary as hell, believe me."

And when his passengers looked where his motioning head was pointing the accident had happened, they saw a sheer drop-off of several hundred feet almost straight down.

Other cars coming hazardously close to the edges of the road to pass stranded motorists; cars coming down losing their brakes; tires coming off and spinning past autos coming up, were more of his tales. All narratives were told with a twinkling eye constantly looking back in the rearview mirror to his passengers to see how they were reacting to the telling of these horror stories.

He then made a point of letting his tourists know he never told these stories on the way up, "For obvious reasons," he stated. "No one would want to ride back down with me if I did, and really, folks, we've had no fatalities in the two years I've been driving... close calls I have to admit, but not one fatality."

They made it back to the parking lot without an incident, with much merriment and jesting back and forth, the sights of the beautiful scenery still assailing their visual recollections.

Even the memory of the dizzying height made Cathy feel slightly woozy when she recalled the views.

It's too good to be true, Cathy thought. Joe has not been called for one of his 'trips' for several weeks. She held her breath at times when she stopped to think about it, so she tried very hard not to think or worry about it....

CHAPTER SIX

For several days Cathy had noticed a want-ad placed in the newspaper that interested her. She had torn it out, read it and reread it many times each day, sometimes with an intense interest, and then with an, 'Oh, what am I thinking of', attitude.

It was an advertisement saying: 'EARN AS YOU LEARN AS AN X-RAY TECHNICIAN AT MEMORIAL HOSPITAL.' It declared that a student would be paid a stipend to learn the profession of x-ray technology, and at the end of two years would be eligible to take the Board Exam to become a licensed x-ray technician.

'BEGINNING AT $60.00 A MONTH, YOU WILL LEARN HOW TO TAKE ALL X-RAYS AND THE TECHNICALITIES OF THE PROFESSION. A STUDENT COULD START AS SOON AS POSSIBLE', and a telephone number was included.

X-ray tech. Cathy Cabal, X-Ray Technician, Cathy mused, liking the sound of it. Hmmm, doesn't sound too bad. I don't want to do nursing or lab work, but have always liked the idea of working in the medical field. Maybe this is my chance to do that. X-ray technology sounds kind of... good, somehow. Think I'll call and see what the deal is and when I would be able to start.

She called and set up an interview on the following Wednesday afternoon at one p.m. at the personnel office of the hospital. "It's on the second floor," she was told.

When she arrived she was given a data sheet to fill out of her work experience, and pertinent information of her personal history; year born and where, color of hair and eyes, what sex, race, and nationality, and two personal references. Cathy quickly finished writing and returned it to the personnel manager, who promptly took her into an office for the interview.

"Have you ever worked in a hospital before, Miss Cabal?"

"No, M'am, but I've always liked the idea of working in the medical field. I just couldn't afford to pay for schooling, and that's why this really appeals to me... that I could be paid while learning, I mean," Cathy replied. "When I considered the job, I knew I didn't want to do nursing or lab work. This is a wonderful alternative and I'd really like to learn x-ray. Know nothing about it, have never had an x-ray or anything except for the fluoroscope machines that a shoe store used to check how shoes fit. But that was when I was younger."

"Well, your work record and all other criteria meet our requirement, so let me take you to see Helen Mosey, who is the technician in charge of the x-ray department. She'll have the final say anyway."

She then made a quick telephone call to ascertain that Helen was there, then stood up, and motioned for Cathy to follow.

Mrs. Templeton led her along a long corridor and down the steps to the main floor, then followed another hallway leading to the office of the x-ray department.

Mrs. Templeton ushered Cathy in, then followed her into the room. Helen Mosey was busy at her desk typing what looked to be some kind of report. When she swiveled around and stood up Cathy perceived a tall, slender, dark-haired young woman of about 28-30 years of age, whose plastic-framed glasses hugged her nose.

"Helen, this is Miss Cathy Cabal. Cathy, Miss Mosey."

"Hello. Do you type, Cathy?" Helen asked very bluntly.

"Hello, yes, but not very fast right now. I haven't been practicing very much lately," Cathy answered as she shook Helen's hand.

"Well, the job includes typing reports the radiologist dictates on our patients' exams," her hand swept toward the typewriter. "That's what I've been doing just now. We also do electrocardiograms from this department known as EKG's. That's not too difficult to learn though. When you get trained enough in everything, you'll be expected to take emergency call, rotating with Shirley, my second year student, and myself, so it would only be every third week. You'll receive an extra $2.00 a day pay for every night you're on call which includes the weekend." All the while her eyes swept Cathy up and down.

Taking a deep breath, she continued, "Our workweek is Monday through Friday, with call every night from the end of workday to beginning of next workday, and through Saturday and Sunday until 7 a.m. Monday morning. Does all this still interest you? Do you have any questions?"

Helen's not one to beat around the bush about anything, Cathy observed. She seems to be a very busy technician who is short of help and can't take a lot of time fooling around.

With her head swimming from the information given her, she could only think of one question. "How long would I train before I would have to start taking call, and exactly what does that mean?"

"Probably about three months. That's about the average length of time you'd need before feeling confident enough to be on your own," Helen answered. "We don't have formal classes, but we have all the books you'll require for your study and use. And Shirley or I will be available to answer your questions and to train you on how to do the exams. And 'call' means doing emergency work that comes in through the night."

Cathy tried to think ahead. "I live in an apartment across town and have no car. Do you know of any apartments or rooms available close by that I could rent? It would have to be within a short walking distance for call, wouldn't it?"

"Yep, there are rooms very close around here that the medical residents sometime stay at and are usually very reasonably priced. If you have a problem and can't find anything close enough, when you're on call you stay in the hospital; there are rooms on the top floor that are available for that for the personnel. In really bad weather, I've stayed here many times myself."

"Ahem," Mrs. Templeton cleared her throat and interjected, "Perhaps you would like to see Miss Cabal's file that I've brought along?"

Helen took it and glanced through it swiftly and asked Mrs. Templeton if she could see her privately a few minutes.

Excusing themselves, the two disappeared into a room directly off the office; a room that looked to be full of equipment and a large dark table of some kind from the quick glance Cathy had when the door was opened briefly.

"Wow, this is happening fast," Cathy reflected.

She went over and over the things Helen had told her, trying to remember everything said, then looked deep within herself.

Am I ready for this kind of commitment? What if I'm not ready to spend time and hours studying and working at a career I know nothing about as yet? What if it doesn't fit me?" 'What if's' were flying through her thoughts right and left, and then the big 'what if'... What if I don't do it, will I regret it? What if I don't get the offer of the position? Suddenly the last 'what if' seemed to be a horrible thought. Not get the job? This thought almost crushed Cathy.

Maybe this is something I was meant to do the way I already seem to feel about it, she thought. Anyway, I'll soon find out.

Looking around the office she waited for Mrs. Templeton and Helen to return.

She glanced curiously at the report Helen had been working on still in the typewriter. Most of the medical terms meant nothing to her. 'Small bowel' she recognized, but 'duodenum', jejunum', barium sulfate', ulceration of', were words that stimulated her fascination. How the doctor found the things these words were describing she couldn't even guess. This seems to be an exciting field of medical discovery, she thought. To be able to see into a patients' body and record these unusual findings on an x-ray film! These imaginations suddenly excited her interest enough to be the thing Cathy wanted to do more than anything she could think of.

When Mrs. Templeton and Helen returned to the office, Cathy had a funny feeling in the pit of her stomach, but they only said they would let her know in a couple of days. They wanted to check her references first and would call her.

Wait it out. Be patient. Joe called that night while she was at work, and she relayed what had happened that day. "Joe, I'm afraid I'm not going to get the job about as much afraid if I do get it. Am I crazy, or what?" she fretted to him.

He did his best to placate her and soothe her fears.

"Princess, if you get it, you were meant to have it and you'll do a good job; if you don't get the offer, you'll have to seek an alternative if this is what you believe you really want to do.

Take it one step at a time, sweet one. Try not to worry about it too much, okay?"

But the next couple of days were very anxious ones for her.

The following Monday, Mrs. Templeton called Cathy at home, and offered her the job. "When can you start, Miss Cabal?"

"I'll give my one-week notice at the restaurant as soon as I hang up right now, Mrs. Templeton. I'll be able to start one week from today then. And thank you very much."

Excitedly, she made her obligatory call to the manager at the restaurant, and then tried to call Joe, leaving a message at the NCO club, asking 'Griz' if he could get word to him somehow. The corporal promised he would try.

But Joe never called. He was gone again, Cathy speculated, and she felt her heart and insides being pulled apart; Hank must be gone also. Why! Why is he doing this to me! Doesn't he know what he's doing to me when he disappears like this?" She cried, she threw pillows and towels around her apartment in angry bursts of frustration. But she knew there was no way of changing it.

She went on about her business, the pursuit of finding a room she could afford on a budget of Sixty Dollars a month. She did have some meager savings put back, but didn't want to dig into those unless it was absolutely necessary.

Across the street from the front entrance to the hospital was a sleeping room advertised with a sign on the front lawn. A widowed elderly lady rented out the room to medical personnel, and luck was with Cathy. It came with a tiny refrigerator, private bathroom, and a very comfortable-looking single bed in a sparsely decorated small bedroom. There was only the one front entrance to the house, and it rented for only Thirty Dollars a month. No cooking was allowed, but the tiny fridge could keep cold drinks, milk, sandwich meat, cheese or snack foods.

Cathy found it difficult to believe her luck, and it was only when she explained to the owner, Mrs. Sees, what she was going to be doing that the frail and white-haired lady told her, "Shirley stayed with me the first few months of her training. But when she kept bringing her rowdy friends over, I had to ask her to leave. I'm not against anyone having friends over, mind you, Miss Cabal," she hastily added, "but they kept helping themselves to things in my refrigerator, and putting their dirty boots up on my furniture and tearing things up. I didn't really like them very much."

Cathy would later find out that Shirley loved rodeo's and all that went with them. She did wild Brahma bull-riding and some bronco-busting on her time off and was into the rodeo scene very deeply. The friends she had brought to Mrs Sees house were cowboys with the rodeo's that played heavily to big screaming crowds in the Springs Rodeo Grounds every Friday and Saturday night.

With her final paycheck from the restaurant, Cathy went shopping and bought her first all-white uniform, white hose and shoes, taking everything back to the room. Her friends from Cosmos had helped her move, and get the things she needed organized in her tiny room.

"It seems to be a tad bit crowded in here, doesn't it?" she worried. "I'll just leave a lot of it in the boxes for now since I don't have any space for some of this junk. Maybe Mrs Sees has a storage area I can rent or use." With that thought in mind, she went to the kitchen where the landlady was enjoying a cup of tea and reading a romance novel.

"Oh, yes, my dear," the lady told her, "I have a small area in the attic you can store some of your boxes if you need to, and you can get to them anytime you want because the attic entrance is in your closet."

Using a chair to stand on, Cathy found a small, sectioned, wooden ladder attached above the hinged ceiling door. She unfolded it, and made sure it was securely on the floor and the small boxes were then very easily carried up and into the space.

It really wasn't too much of an inconvenience to have to move the few clothes hanging on the rod to get to the attic door, as Cathy's clothes were sorted for this summer season and all others packed away.

With that chore done, Cathy said," Hey, everyone. I want to treat you to thank you for helping me move. Mrs Sees, what's nearby?"

They decided on a local root beer stand they had spotted for hot dogs and root beer floats. They crowded joyously into Jill's car and took off, having persuaded Mrs Sees to join them.

Mrs Sees protested, "I'll have some root beer, but no hot dog for me, thank you."

And in a conspiratorial whisper to Cathy, "They don't always agree with me, you know."

Cathy smiled in the seeming conspiracy and assured her, "You may have whatever you wish."

CHAPTER SEVEN

The next day she reported promptly at 7 a.m. to the x-ray department. She was taken to an exam room and handed a heavy apron to put on and instructed to stand behind a narrow, stubby wall with a small window in it to observe the procedure of fluoroscopy that Dr Anderson was doing on a patient.

Helen told her, "Dr Anderson is doing a 'G.I.' study, which stands for 'Gastro-Intestinal', stomach exam. The apron and walls are lined with lead to protect those of us who work in it all the time from too much radiation. Dr Anderson wears a lead apron also."

The patient, a very thin-looking elderly woman in a white cotton long hospital wraparound gown, was standing on a foot-piece attached to one end of the x-ray table which was in an upright position. Shirley gave the lady a glass of white chalky-looking liquid that Cathy had watched being mixed earlier in the workroom.

The radiologist ordered, "Take two swallows, M'am."

As Cathy watched, there was a faint gray shadow that moved on the yellow glowing screen Dr Anderson was maneuvering about in front of the woman.

Helen said, "The shadow is the white liquid barium going down the patients' throat and into her stomach; doctor is watching as it moves and examining her esophagus to see if it's all right also."

As he scanned, Dr Anderson told the patient to take more of the white barium from the glass, and he then, at the push of a button, started the table moving backwards to the flat position as he studied the screen. He had the lady turn from side to side, taking x-ray pictures as he examined her abdomen.

After the doctor had finished, he placed goggles fully enclosed with red lenses on his face that fully protected his eyes from any white light, and went to his office as Shirley and Helen then proceeded with the examination, taking several more x-ray pictures using an overhead camera that was suspended from the ceiling.

When they had finished Helen said, "Relax for a few minutes, Mrs Webster, while we check the films."

Helen then escorted Cathy into the darkroom. The only light was the illumination from a small bulb in an enclosed box with a red filter; this box hung above the counter and allowed only a faint red glow within the room. She proceeded to remove each film from its cassette and manually processed each in and out of the prescribed solutions as needed.

When the processing was done, she dunked them up and down several times in a water bath, gathered them together and with a protective towel under them to catch the drips, took them to Dr Anderson for his final approval. They did show the abnormality in the patients' abdomen he wanted to demonstrate. Mrs Webster was then helped into the dressing room and told to go ahead and get dressed, her exam was completed.Setting the wet films back into the wash tank and going back into the examining room Cathy was allowed to stand closer to the radiologist this time so she could see more clearly what he was doing and seeing as he explained and pointed out to her different parts of the patients' anatomy on his screen.

She watched another of the G. I. exams being done, and then gasped through an exam of the lower bowel with the encompassing barium enema, the gentleman grunting with pain and discomfort as they proceeded.

It was exciting, fascinating, almost supernatural the way Cathy felt about those first couple hours of her first day.

The telephone kept jangling its incessant sound, and picking it up this time, Helen listened to the voice on the other end.

"Need you in ER 'STAT', Helen. Portable chest x-ray and EKG."

Helen repeated the message to Cathy and, motioning for her to follow, took an x-ray cassette from the wall Pass-through and headed for the portable x-ray unit stored in a nearby hall alcove. Pushing the smaller EKG unit, that was also stored there, towards Cathy, she brusquely ordered Cathy to follow her with it, and hurried down the hallway toward the emergency room; Helen wheeled the large unit very confidently into the room.

The patient was an older, gray-haired, very large and smooth-skinned gentleman with an oxygen mask over his mouth and nose. Tubes from his arms and nose draped and fell across his chest and large belly in helter-skelter profusion. He was in a semi-reclining position and gasping for every available breath he could get, his dark eyes flitting back and forth around the room. His visible body from the waist up was ashen gray in pallor, and moisture glistened as a clammy perspiration ran off his face. A sheet shielded his lower body and legs.

Doctors and nurses were calmly, yet hurriedly, moving over him, with blood pressure cuffs inflating, and then deflating their hissing messages into the ears that were connected by stethoscopes to the panting life.

Needles, flashing and glittering in the bright lights, were attached to syringes with hopeful heart restoration serums and solutions that were injected into the lifelines of tubes in the patients' arm at the soft-voiced command of a man standing nearby.

Never having seen an ensemble such as this before, Cathy stood in awe, and some fear, outside the doorway as Helen maneuvered the machine alongside the gurney and plugged the unit into an outlet. The nurses helped her sit him up enough to slip the cassette behind his back and then rested him back on it, the coldness of it bringing a gasp and shudder from the patient.

She quickly positioned her x-ray tube in front and above him, explaining to Cathy she had to keep the film and tube parallel to each other, and measured a forty-inch distance with a metal tape leading from the edge of the x-ray tube carrier.

She shouted, "X-ray on!" when she was ready to make the exposure, and she motioned with her hand for Cathy to get out of the room. All personnel moved quickly and temporarily behind doors or walls, or whatever was closest to them, for shelter from the scatter radiation. In seconds, the x-ray was taken and nurses again rushed to aid her to again raise the patient and remove the cassette.

Handing the cassette to Cathy Helen brusquely ordered her to, "Take it back to Shirley to process, get a report from Dr Anderson, and then bring it and the report back to the emergency room."

As she was talking to Cathy, Helen had manipulated the big x-ray machine out of the room and took in the smaller EKG unit.

"Give the film and report to Dr Costas over there, Cathy," Helen instructed her, "Wait until they're finished with the film, then take it back and put it into the water-bath." She was moving swiftly about her job as she talked.

As Cathy was walking away, she saw Helen put a gel-like substance from a tube onto a small area of the skin on the inside of the patients' ankles.

Apprehensively, Cathy did as she was instructed, and later when walking back into the emergency room she didn't know which doctor was the Dr Costas she was to report to. Holding the film up she quietly announced, "I'm back with the film. Who do I show this to?" A nurse standing nearby motioned with her head across the room.

"Over here! Over here!" an impatient voice beckoned, and an arm raised high signaled her to a side alcove where the view-box was. She hastily moved across the brightly lit room toward the alcove and handed the dripping film to a very tall young man with golden-curly hair on exposed wrists, and long agile fingers at the end of very powerful looking hands. A wisp of longish blonde, also curly, hair strayed from under the large blue cotton surgical cap, and it tried to reach down and tease the tips of the brown-gold lashes that surrounded his worried doe-like brown eyes.

The blue cotton pullover scrub-top he wore was stuffed into blue cotton scrub pants, tied with a pull closure, and over this pairing he wore a starched white lab coat, the sleeves very much shorter than his golden arms as he held the film high on the view-box to study it.

She handed the hastily handwritten report to him.

Glancing at it, he nodded, and grumbled, "Humph, just as I suspected, grossly enlarged heart, pneumonia in lungs. Good Lord, it's a wonder he's made it as long as he has. He's full of edema, blood pressures' sky high, kidney's shutting down...."

Very dejectedly, "Okay, that's all I need. Thanks," as he handed the film back and nodded his dismissal to Cathy.

She took the film from him and scurried out of the room, looking quickly at the man again as she passed him, seeing now from a totally different context the patient on the special bed.

This is a man, Cathy suddenly realized, who seems to be dying, and there isn't a lot anyone can do for him except make him as comfortable as possible for the time he has left. She shuddered as the thought crossed her mind, and she determined to think more about it.

She gave the film to Shirley, went to the office and sat down at the desk, suddenly shaking, wondering if she really knew what she was getting into.

"This had been a harrowing experience for the very first morning of a medical career," she pondered.

Most of the rest of the day was spent in 'routine' examinations doing spine, heads, shoulders, arms, and legs in the department, some from car accidents, some from falls, fights, and children falling out of swings, along with a couple more portable chest x-rays and EKG's on other newly admitted patients.

It was late afternoon when Cathy first saw this one particular young man. He was sitting on the end of the x-ray table, his eyes glaring an insolence that would not allow him to even acknowledge his pain. When she glanced at his papers, she found he was a young 22-year-old prisoner from the county jail, brought in to find the bullet in his shoulder from his having tried to elude the police at a transfer point.

He sat, straight as an arrow as Helen brought the x-ray tube in front of him. He looked directly at Cathy and said, "Call me 'Billy the Kid'." The prisoner was unable to lie down on the table because of the bone fragment projecting through the skin in the front of the shoulder; Helen had explained lying down could have been very hazardous, with the possibility of rupturing a large blood vessel.

He really scared Cathy with his seeming attitude of, 'I dare you to hurt me any more!' His eyes were cold and hard with eyebrows tightly gathered in furrows over them. She felt very upset for him.

The end of the day was welcome relief to Cathy. Helen had taken the time to bring out a couple of anatomy and x-ray positioning textbooks. "Cathy, these are the latest and best books available to learn from. Study them! I don't expect you to understand all you're looking at right away, but take your time, ask questions for explanations. Start with the extremities of hands and feet, and learn forward and backward the anatomy you'll be expected to know. There's a full-body bone skeleton hanging in Dr Anderson's office you can study from also."

She continued, "Oh, and by the way, Cathy, every once in a while, I'll be giving you quizzes on anatomy and positioning. Very informal, very loose and no grading, but important that you know what to be expecting on a Board Exam in two years."

Cathy was exhausted and drained... emotionally, as well as physically. I thought I was in better shape than this, for Pete sake!

The heart-rending difficulty of witnessing a dying person today opened the floodgate of memories on the death of her father. He had not died as this man was most likely to, but she was present at his passing. His had been peaceful, albeit until the very last hour a defiance and hope had been bright in his brown eyes.

Cathy struggled to understand and achieve some perspective about her new undertaking. This man today, she thought, a frown creasing her forehead, now I know this is bound to happen again and again, and I'm going to have to learn to control the situation, or I'm going to be doomed in this job before ever getting started. Maybe it's a darn good thing this happened my first day, get thrown in the ring full blast, so-to-speak.

Her thoughts continued, questioning. Is this what's called 'being professional'? Be compassionate, do your job, treat all patients humanely and still keep a safe emotional distance? I wonder. It seems this is what everyone I observed today was doing. The doctor was obviously worried, yet issued his orders in the manner befitting a commander in charge of his army. The nurses struggled to ease the man's pain, their touch gentle and empathetic, yet firm and in control.

And, I'll have to talk about this to Helen tomorrow——feel pretty confused about how you do all these things. Damn, I wish Joe were here to talk to; he's a professional soldier, but I'd bet he could give me some insight into this.

With these thoughts racing through her, Cathy fixed a sandwich and opened a bottle of orange juice. As she ate and drank, she turned the light on over the small table in the corner of her room and cracked open the textbook of anatomy.

CHAPTER EIGHT

he days of the next week were a frenzied whirlwind. Cathy determinedly cracked open her books each night, and gave thanks she had them to fall upon with Joe still gone. She blistered Helen and Shirley's' ears each day with questions and dogged their heels at their every move, sometimes taking the x-ray positioning book into the control booth with her to better visualize what they were doing in the actual exam.

She stayed after the others had gone, after the department was closed, to clean the equipment from the mire and spatters that happen with sick and injured patients, and found she didn't mind that at all. It helped her to get the feel of each camera and stand, as she moved them back and forth on their overhead tracks.

The cold metal of the x-ray table seemed to give her a feeling of awesome… what? Power? Humility? Having the potential of holding a person's wellbeing in your hands can be unnerving. She should have been feeling guilty because she didn't really have the time or energy to worry and fuss about Joe or Hank. Through that first week it was a never-ending blur of early rising, work, study, exhausted sleep, then restart the cycle.

She persisted, and friends from Cosmos stopped by her room that weekend to cheer her on, and to boost her morale.

The second and third week were the same, until Thursday night of that third week.

When she walked back to her room, Joe was sitting out front in his Chevy waiting for her; he had found out where she was from her friends at the restaurant. She ran to him calling his name. He stepped out of the car and caught her in a joyous embrace, raining kisses on her lips, face, hair, and holding her as though he never wanted to let go. She cried his name over and over, and molded and wiggled herself into his arms as close as she could get.

He was in uniform this time, and when she stood back finally to look at him closely, she exclaimed in alarm. "Joe, are you all right? You look like you haven't slept the whole time you've been gone. Sweet one, come on in and have a cup of coffee, and we'll talk. I want to tell you all about my new job," knowing full well they wouldn't be talking about his.

"So far, I love it." She took his arm and began to guide him to the front entrance as she talked.

She swept her hand in a grand gesture to the one and only reclining easy chair in her room, "Have a seat," and watched as he sat exhaustedly down.

She busied herself with the percolator. "Seesie has allowed me to make coffee in my room. She says she doesn't believe that really constitutes 'cooking', and I really need it in the morning to get my eyes open. It won't take long, and..." As she had glanced over her shoulder at Joe she stopped midway in her sentence, "Oh, dear...." when she saw he was fast asleep, his legs stretched out and his head rolled to his left shoulder against the back of the cushioned recliner.

Cathy felt hot tears of tenderness, and then anger, sting her eyes. "Oh, dammit! What's he been doing while he's been gone? He's evidently totally exhausted, and I can't know what brought him to this point. I only know I'm so glad he's back now. She put a lightweight blanket across him, lovingly touched his cheek with her lips. Then with the thought that Seesie might misunderstand a soldier asleep in her room, she sought out her landlady in the kitchen and asked if she might study in the living room for awhile and with honesty told her why. She left the door to her room open so as to be able to glance at him.

"I'll wake him at ten o'clock, Seesie, I promise, if he doesn't wake before then," Cathy pledged.

Joe was awake again in an hour, seemingly refreshed and feeling better, but slightly chagrined.

Cathy had finished making the pot of coffee, and now offered him some of the steaming brew. "Joe, are you okay now?" she whispered softly.

"Sure, Cathy. Feel rather embarrassed I fell asleep in your chair but do appreciate you letting me sleep for awhile.

Had a long flight, and...." Joe interrupted himself and apologized again in a rather charming sheepish way.

"I'm sorry. I believe I'd better be on my way while I'm awake enough to drive back to base. The coffee helps a lot, thanks. And goodnight, Mrs Sees," he waved in the direction of the kitchen. "Thanks for allowing me to rest for awhile."

Cathy kissed him lightly and gave him a tight hug. "Drive very carefully on the way back, you."

He touched the back of his right hand against her chin, then tilted her face up again with those fingers and kissed her a feather touch on the lips.

"I promise," he whispered. "Will I see you this weekend?"

"Yes, why don't we get Hank and Glenna and go out to dinner somewhere and a movie, and just get together and have a good time," suggested Cathy.

He dropped his bombshell very quietly. "One good reason is because Hank didn't come home with me. He's in a hospital in Tokyo."

"Ohmygod, Joe, what happened? Is he going to be all right?" Cathy panicked immediately, her voice and emotional reaction triggered with the thought of seriously injured Hank—alone—in a foreign hospital..

She stamped her foot hard on the carpet, "Joe, tell me, what happened. Tell me before I explode."

"All right, Cathy, calm down, calm down. He's going to be okay. He has a couple of broken bones that are just going to take time, otherwise, he's fine. No major internal injuries or anything like that. He'll probably be home in a couple of weeks. I've already talked to Glenna and told her. She's trying to figure out a way to go be with him for awhile, but she doesn't know if she can swing it or not. She's a nervous wreck."

"And," very sarcastically from Cathy, "of course, you can't tell me how or where he got hurt, can you?"

"No, but does it matter that much?" A very low, calm voice.

Her voice rose with utter frustration, "Were you with him? Could that just as well have been you?"

"Come on, Cathy, you know I can't tell you anything," said still so icily soft.

"Can't, and won't, yes, I know," muttered a suddenly subdued and regretful Cathy. "I'm sorry, I shouldn't have taken that tone with you, Joe, but it scares me to think, it could be you there in that hospital bed."

"I know, Princess. It could have been." And hesitantly, "Are you going to be all right? Think I'd better be on my way now. We'll talk more this weekend." Joe had been holding her hands in his, and he brought them to his lips, put a caressing touch of a kiss on each, and turned to leave. "Why don't I call you tomorrow night and we'll figure out what to do this weekend."

"Yes, and I'm going to call Glenna and see how she's doing. Maybe just talking might help her. Goodnight, Joe."

Cathy was on the phone almost immediately and talking to a tearful Glenna. "Glenna, Joe's told me Hank's going to be alright. Just things that will take a while to heal before he can come back home. He said you were going to try and go there. Are you going to make it?"

"No, I just don't have that kind of money to make that kind of a trip. I called him and talked to him on the phone, and he sounds the same, but kind-of depressed, ya' know?" Glenna responded. "Trying to get a call through to that city into the hospital was a nightmare of red tape you wouldn't believe. I think a carrier pigeon could have done as well, so doubt I'll do that again. He did give me an address to write to, so I'll do that."

"Well, if I can help you in any way, please let me know," a supportive Cathy stated.

That Saturday when Joe came to pick up Cathy to go for a drive, he seemed very quiet, curt, and withdrawn. Without a word to her he headed the car into the mountains. They had gone a long distance in a silent and unusually uncomfortable tension.

Cathy tried several different times to promote a conversation, but only received short grunts, or a quick shrug of shoulders from Joe. When he pulled into an overlook that harbored a beautiful view of a creek and valley which channeled your eyes toward a small community lying far below, Cathy felt an immediate apprehension.

Getting out of the car, he walked towards the chain-link fence and gazed moodily toward the village spread out before him, not really seeing the view at all, the muscles in his clenched jaw rippling.

Cathy followed slowly, "Joe, what's the matter? You haven't said two words since we left the apartment."

"I'm going back to Tokyo tomorrow morning." Blunt, to the point, and terrifying to Cathy's ears, and with the shock of the words, her jaw clamped tight, and she could barely get her breath.

As the long moment of silence strung out from Cathy, she tried to get control of her tumbling heart, and a fear settled over her like an impenetrable, ashen cloud, crushing all vision of anything around her—except Joe. Scared to death. Too afraid to make a sound.

Cathy finally could squeeze the words out past her barely controlled choking voice. "Why, to be with Hank? I thought you said he was going to be all right."

Joe responded very hesitantly, cautiously, "He's going to be all right. It's just that someone needs to... help him because he's very... vulnerable right now."

A long pulsating pause that was filled with the sounds of the passing traffic, the moan of a train whistle somewhere, and the warmth of the breeze lightly whipping at their clothes. He still leaned against the fence for support but turned to her momentarily.

"You know, it's not like I was going on the other 'trip,'" he hotly contested.

"Besides, Command says someone should be there, and I'm just the one who's been told to go." He turned his eyes back to the valley, but saw nothing.

Cathy burst out loudly. "By 'vulnerable', and 'needs help' you mean he knows too much, he's helpless, and there are a lot of unscrupulous people out there who might take advantage of that fact. Am I close?" She was feeling defenseless, powerless. Irritated.

Joe turned his gaze on her again and squinted his eyes in appraisal of what she seemingly understood the situation to be.

He droned in a very controlled voice, "He hasn't been alone. There's always been someone with him, but that guy has been called back to the States. His wife was in a very bad car accident."

He turned away again.

"Sweet one," Cathy continued, more softly now as she moved up behind him and put her arms around his waist, still trying to be optimistic. "If you need to be with Hank to protect him and take care of him, I think that's terrific. If this is the case all of us would breathe easier knowing you're there. I would, you would, and so would Glenna."

Joe pivoted around within her light grasp and with a sweeping move pulled her tightly into his arms, hugging her close, rocking her back and forth within those enclosing arms that made up the circle of her life.

"Princess..., Cathy!" He seemed unable to say what he wanted to. His face, when she glanced up at him, was contorted and tight, his jaw tightly clamped.

"Hey, Joe, don't misunderstand, please. I don't want you to leave at all, period, but at least it's not the other job, and I also know you're not going to rest easy until Hank gets home safely. So, dear one, go, and get him and yourself home as quickly as you can." She squeezed him tightly, savoring the strength of his firm, consoling arms around her.

He moved with her to the side of the little cove into the shadows of an over-hanging tree and kissed her, hungrily, greedily, his strong parted lips moving and pressing hard as he had never kissed her before. His tongue scorched the inside of her mouth. He held her possessively, his hands tensely stroking her back and hips, urgently pulling her into him as never before; the heat of his desire almost impelling them to forget where they were.

Cathy felt this urgency, and returned kiss for kiss, her hands also stroking the hardness of his neck, shoulders, and rippling back muscles. The fire that was started within her entire body courted disaster with her control. The emotional rollercoaster of her need for him, and the fact that tomorrow he was going to be gone for a few weeks again almost, but not quite, sanctioned her giving in to whatever would happen.

It was Joe who backed off, who stopped the whirlwinds, trumpets and rockets that were blasting their way through each one. He had sensed her infinitesimal pulling away, and almost belatedly, remembered where they were. Trembling and shaking, breathing heavily, he loosened his hold slightly on her. He gazed at her with those blue pools Cathy loved; eyes that were not blue now, but full of the pain and anguish that burned and darkened them like coal that has been turned to dusky sooty-gray.

With a sudden and chilling insight, Cathy said, "There's more, isn't there, Joe; more you're going to tell me." She stood so still in his arms, her entire being suddenly drained of all power to move.

"I won't be coming back to the States, sweet Princess." He was making the words come out, but Cathy wasn't understanding any of them.

He stepped backwards, away from her and then turned his back to her, and grabbed the top of the fence again as though he couldn't bear to look at her, to see the distress in her eyes.

She was very puzzled, "What do you mean, Joe, you won't be coming back to the States'?"

"From Tokyo, I'll be going to another base, in Europe." A fertile suspense grew with each passing second. Then a deep, resolute sigh, "I've been transferred."

Very agitated, his mouth a thin tight line when he turned to look at her. He paused, studying her a moment, then continued. "Cathy, it's better this is happening now. Do you remember when we first met I said I'd probably live to regret allowing myself to get to know you? Well, sweetheart, the regrets have already begun. I leave at 7:10 tomorrow morning and we'll not be seeing each other again for a very long time, if ever, and it's tearing me up. But it has to be."

His voice rose, "You must remember, and I wanted to forget, intensely, that I'm married to this damnable job and the Army, and have no space there for any other fulltime civilian commitment. And you..., you, sweet Cathy," he groaned, "deserve no less than that." In his despair, he kicked at a stone which seemed to be in his way in front of his foot, sending it skittering and rolling down the slight hillside they were on and onto the highway beside them.

Cathy was incredulous. "All this happened since I saw you day before yesterday?"

"Yeh, I'm afraid so," he replied sourly.

Her voice was stinging and rising in anger. She was in pain, numb, sickened, all at the same time, barely able to mouth her words, "You just take off and I have to accept it, is that it?"

He turned away again to keep from looking at her and from her seeing his face.

Her utterance of, "Take me home, Joe, please," was drenched with misery.

Somehow, deep in her heart she had known this day could happen. She just never let herself believe it would.

"Cathy, I... I'm sorry." He looked at her then, and she knew he was feeling as much pain; his distress mirroring her own; his tears matching hers.

They retreated to the car and he headed it reluctantly towards the city.

Desperately, she tried to talk about anything just to keep from screaming.

"What about Hank, Joe? Is he in the same situation? Is Glenna hoping for something she's never going to have also, Joe? Is that how this works?"

He grumbled testily, "I don't know. He'll probably come home for therapy for awhile. Where he goes or what happens then is up to the powers that be."

He took her home and on arriving at the door, they looked at each other long and hard, agonizingly trying to tell each other without words that what was happening wasn't true. Words couldn't come. But she knew. Oh, God, how the pain in her heart knew!

And she knew, also, she had to let him go.

She finally managed through quivering lips, "Joe, I want to come see you off tomorrow morning."

"No, Cathy, please don't. I couldn't say goodbye twice. This time is bad enough," he implored.

He kissed her softly, lovingly, daring not to envelop her in his arms again as he longed to. He stepped away, turned and walked down the sidewalk towards the car.

She stood there, overcome, icy to her inner core. When she could breathe again, her feet finally took her at a run down the sidewalk crying loudly his name, "Joe!................Joe!"

Flinging herself into his outstretched arms, she clung to him with arms tight around his neck, sobbing, burying her face into his shoulder, then against his face, their tears to be the only part of them to ever intertwine. He held her, lifted her, and stumbled backward a step or two against the car.

"Please take care of yourself, Joe. Promise me you'll keep your mind on your job when you're doing one, and stay safe. Promise me, please!" she pleaded with him between sobs, "And will you, somehow, let me know how Hank's doing... through Glenna, through Hank... just somehow, tell them, let me know." Let me know how you are, my love.

Very agitated, "Do you really have to go?" The look on his face told her. "I'll pray for both of you."

She reached to her throat and tore off a small gold neck-chain with a tiny gold heart pendant and dropped it into his shirt pocket. Breathlessly, tremulously, "Take this to remember me, Joe. Remember me as I'll always treasure you."

Her lips found his then and she frantically tried to cling to him, but he groaned, a guttural sound coming from deep within him, pulled her arms from his neck and pushed her gently but very firmly away from him. He touched her face with his hand, turned, went quickly around to the driver side, and was gone in a searing moment in the dark blue Chevy.

She walked into the house to her room in a daze, closed the door, and sat without seeing, without feeling, without knowing the day had turned to night and she was sitting in the dark.

Only when the light rays of dawn began to encroach upon her numbed consciousness did she stir from the chair. Going into the bathroom and throwing cold water onto her face she hastily combed her hair, retouched her lipstick and went to the telephone and called a cab.

"The airport, please, driver," she heard herself say.

She had no sense of transitional movement as the taxi swung itself through the dawn light. Once there, she had the driver let her out along the outer fence that bordered the concourse where the plane was parked. She could see the plane, and the space where the passengers had to walk from the terminal to get to it was long enough and close enough that she'd be able to see him.

Then she waited, her face pressed against the cold chain-link fence, peering through it and watching every movement of the people from the terminal. Finally, a long line of humanity started straggling out of the building heading toward the airplane.

The sun was beginning to peep through the low horizon clouds and a shaft of light splintered onto the fence and onto her face, and at the same moment a transient cool breeze made her shudder.

Squinting against the momentary brightness she saw.... Yes, there he is. He's really going, he really is! Oh, Joe, why! Why us? Why couldn't we have a life together like others do? She moaned softly, tears shimmering her eyes.

It was strange; he stopped in mid-walk as though he heard her moan of distress. He shook his head slightly and then moved on up the stairs toward the cavity that gaped before him. When he reached the top of the steps, he stopped again, turned and looked toward where he felt the magnetism of her grief. She could never know the shock of yearning that slammed through him when he caught sight of a silhouette, another transient shaft of sun having captured a form on the other side of the fence.

My Princess is, isn't she? standing behind the fence. He paused, his eyes searching, seeking, stretching toward the fence while others moved around him, but the shadows came once again to diffuse and diffract the chain-link fence. He then pivoted quickly and went on inside.

The ray of light that had framed a woman's form cast a spell on his imagining, or was he so full of wishful wanting he had just envisioned her there? He struggled to see that line of fence again, but his seat arrangement, Move... lady... excuse me...get your head out of my way... wouldn't allow him to peer out the window for another look. Dammit. Where is that fence? He reluctantly pacified himself, Yes, it was Cathy. I'm positive!

CHAPTER NINE

Since Joe had been gone, Cathy could only find sleep at night thanks to the help of a newfound friend, a bottle of Vodka spirits. It helped deaden the pain and heartache of the next three months. Vodka was the tranquilizer that soothed her nerves when she wanted to scream at the walls when they closed in on her at night, and it was her companion when she sat in her room studying. The only time she had forsaken it was when she was on duty at the hospital.

She poured herself into learning the craft she had chosen and this week she was to start taking emergency call. Helen had promised to stand by the entire week to help if something came up Cathy didn't know whether she could handle or not. Her confidante, the bottle, called her, but Cathy swore to herself she would not jeopardize her career if she could help it, and resolutely tried to stick to the ultimatum she had given herself.

But would one little swig really hurt?

Somehow, she managed to get through the week, denying her nerves what they needed, and only having to call Helen one time for advice. She then had the entire following weekend free.

Glenna called on Friday. "Hank is in a hospital in New York now, doing well, and I'm flying out on Monday to be with him for a week. He had some setbacks in the Tokyo hospital so was there much longer than expected. He's still doing physical therapy, but almost finished and completely healed. Lots of scarring, as you can imagine, but they don't seem to be bothering him."

Glenna started sniffling and the sound of beginning crying came across the phone. "He told me he would be back to duty in a couple of weeks, but in Europe. He's going to be going to the same outfit with ...." She stopped, not wishing to inflame Cathy's misery, but hoping Cathy understood who she was meaning, her tears and blowing of nose very obvious.

Cathy didn't have the nerve to complete, out loud, the word that Glenna did not finish saying.

So Glenna now knows that he's not coming back here; what's she going to do when Hank's gone? Also, she wondered, is he there yet?

She had stocked up on the bottle, and since she's off-duty took it with her into her room, shut and locked the door, and allowed herself to be lulled into oblivion by the power of the seductive watery-looking liquid.

Later that same night, Cathy hoarsely cried out when the noise and racket finally penetrated through and into her foggy and benumbed brain. "What's all that noise? Who's making all that racket out there...? What do you want?"

Mrs Sees and Jill were pounding on her door and she was being brought up out of the depths of her stupor unwillingly by the two of them calling to her and rattling the door handle.

"Forchrissake Cath, open the damn door. It's Jill. Want to talk to you before I leave."

Annoyed, Cathy tried to struggle to her feet from the recliner, but fell onto the floor alongside the bed, landing with a bumbling sound. It was muffled but enough to be heard along with the grunt and soft-voiced curse, by Jill outside the door.

Dizzily, groggily, her hand to her swirling head, "Go away, Jill. I can't talk right now. I'm...I'm studying." Yeh, that ought to make them go away, ought to send them...away!

In a flash her mood changed, the dizziness eased and Cathy began to giggle very quietly behind her hand, and, "Oopsy-do, I seem to...goodness, I've lost my feet somewhere." Calling lightly now, "Jill? Jill, I seem to have lost my feet somewhere, and I can't study without them." She muttered and searched frantically around her, "All those bones have gotten lost on me. Ohboy ohboy, Helen's going to have my hide if I don't find those feet." Wistfully, her face screwing up to almost tears, "Jill? Are you still there?"

She waited for a moment and heard a commanding, "Yes" coming from the other side of the door.

Then plaintively, and with a deep frustrated sigh, "Please help me find my feet."

"Open the door, Cath, so I can help you," Jill retorted firmly. "You have to unlock the door first."

Cathy crawled to the door, fumbling at the lock that was just above the door-knob and finally managed to turn it open. "I can't find my feet, or I'd stand up to let you in... Oh, hi, Seesie, I din't know you're there. Come'n in, everybody, come'n in and we'll have a party. I'd feel like a party if I could just find my darn feet. Can't have a party without them now, can we?" she said tipsily.

Jill turned to Seesie, "I'll take care of Cathy. Would it be all right if I could make a pot of coffee?"

Seesie looked closely at Cathy, nodded her head at Jill, and left them alone closing the door behind her.

"Come on, Cath, up and at-em. Let's get you in the chair. Okay, now, on three... one, two, heave-ho-three! See, there're your feet; you were sitting on them all the time. Silly you."

Jill was chatting all the while, then began preparing the coffee pot. A hot steaming cup of coffee was what Cathy needed she surmised. Well, perhaps, that and a big lug named Joe.

Jill stayed with Cathy a long time, talked to her, held the coffee mug to her lips to help her drink, and cajoled her into staying awake.

In a severe attitude swing, Cathy suddenly became very hostile toward her. "I don't want to stay awake, Jill, I want to sleep. That way I don't think, or feel, or want to cry and scream." Cathy's lips quivered, her eyes becoming liquid. "I appreciate you being here but go home and let me sleep!"

Jill bit her lip. It was all she could do to keep from crying at seeing what was happening to her friend. "All right, Cath', I'll go for now, but would you go out to dinner with me tonight, just the two of us? Please say you'll go," a worried Jill entreated.

"No, I don't want to go."

"Okay, I'll bring some sandwiches here, and we'll eat in your room," Jill persistently replied.

Cathy stood up turned to Jill, and in a sudden rage screamed, "Jill, leave me alone!"

It was the tremendously hurt expression that passed over Jill's face that caused Cathy to lose control.

"Jill, I'm sorry." And with those almost cleansing words she crumbled in a heap against Jill. The floodgates opened and the tears and anguish Cathy had tried for months to suppress let loose onto Jill's shoulders. Jill held her, handed her tissues, patted her hair, talked softly to her, tears running down her own cheeks.

She sobbed long and hard, the first time since Joe's transfer. The reminder of Hank coming to New York could have been the last straw on her emotional back, and it was a release that was sorely needed. The hysterical merry-go-round of ups and downs she had been on for the past three months could not have lasted much longer. She believed Helen had not suspected her bedfellow, the bottle, as of yet, but it would only be a matter of time. She also knew her work was already beginning to suffer, with ugly hangovers, and fuzzy reacting time with the patients' and radiologist in the x-ray fluoroscopic room.

When she had quieted, Jill handed her another cup of coffee and helped herself to one also; they sat side by side on the edge of the bed sipping the hot brew. Cathy set hers aside after awhile on the table, went into the bathroom and splashed cold water over her face. Coming out of the room, she sat down beside Jill again, her eyes red and swollen, her body more relaxed and slumped.

"I think I'll be okay now, Jill. I really need to be alone for awhile though. Would you mind terribly?"

"No, it's fine with me. Can I get you anything, to eat or something?" she asked, still wiping her own eyes, blowing her nose.

"Thanks, but no, I'm not hungry."

Jill was finally gone.

Cathy looked at the bottle, sitting malignantly on the far corner of the table, walked over to it and in utter contempt and surrender of her self-control, tipped it up into her mouth and swallowed a very large ball of the liquor. She set it down again, walked back to the bed, laid down, and soon slept deep and dreamless through the night.

When she awakened and had had coffee and a sandwich, a single purpose came to her mind; keep her 'friend' to herself.

From now on, she would have to be much more careful. She knew Jill had left for her visit to see Hank and would be gone for a week.

For the next year, she worked as if she walked on the slithering coils of a serpent, working hard at her job each day, and working harder at drowning any feeling after the job was done for the day. She found excuse after excuse not to see anyone, to keep to herself, to mourn by herself the passing of love from her life. The only smiles she had were for the strangers who passed in and out from her care in the x-ray room. Soon, all other acquaintances tired of trying. Cathy found herself, finally, without friendship, without anyone to talk to except the conversations she had with the patients she worked with on her job, and Helen and Shirley. She managed her schedule so she didn't see Seesie, the landlady, either.

They all had busy lives, parties, dating, their own jobs, and the effort to keep Cathy active in their social gatherings became too much for them to tolerate.

Jill was the most persistent and prevailing of her circle of buddies, but before very long, Cathy, instigating a screaming, bombastic quarrel, turned even her away, stabbing Jill with a terrible hurt and feelings of frustration in not being able to help her friend.

The bottle was the only buddy Cathy wanted and she kept her mind and feelings as numb and unaware as she could away from the hospital. Now, there were times when she slipped and her mind was unaware on the job, too. Helen had begun to snap at her irritably, definitely noticing her blunders; and the radiologist had had to speak very sharply many times in the examining room.

He had asked Helen to talk to her, Cathy found out, because his tolerance was worn very thin. Also, Helen's concern for the patient's in Cathy's care prompted her to call Cathy into the office to talk after work on Friday.

"What's going on, Cathy?" Helen started, a warning tone in her voice.

Wide-eyed, not too surprised, but unwilling to acknowledge the possibility of what she meant this time, Cathy reluctantly asked, "What do you mean, Helen?"

Helen shouted, "I mean, what the hell is going on with you! You are inattentive in the examining room, falling asleep in the darkroom, sitting there in the chair when there are exams to be done or reports to type. You know what I mean when I ask you what the hell is going on!"

Helen's displeasure washed over Cathy's soul, causing her to shrink down into the chair, almost physically trying to evade the words she was hearing.

Helen was very angry and distressed, but still saw the utter desolation on Cathy's face. Her voice softened, "You were never like this before, so what gives?"

"I... I need a vacation, Helen," Cathy started tearfully. "I want to go home for awhile...."

A spark of devastation, then a flame of utter desperation hit her and started burning into her soul. "No, on second thought, no vacation, I need to get away from here, period."

She stood up and started to pace back and forth the few steps from chair to Helen's desk. "You have my two-week notice as of this moment, Helen. I can't handle this anymore. I'm going home to my Mom for awhile. I don't think I'm well, and need to leave the Springs and get my health back. Then will take it from there."

Upon seeing Helen's shocked expression, Cathy lamented hurriedly, "It's all my fault, Helen. It's nothing you, or Dr Anderson, or anyone else here has done. You've all been great. It's just... I need a change of scenery. Since Joe's gone, it's become unbearable. I... I just want to go home and rethink my life."

She ended with tears running down her cheeks. It had been a long time since crying the storm on Jill's shoulder, and she felt a resignation and a new determination within her at the finality of moving away and leaving the territory where she had known Joe.

Cathy felt relief to finally be on her way home. To finally have been forced to make the transition from victim of her grief to taking charge again of her life. Relief, and totally consuming sadness.

It was a very difficult two weeks saying goodbye to all those who would even acknowledge her anymore.

Jill did. She cried, and also told her how happy she was that she was finally doing something to take care of herself, even though she was going to miss her friend very much.

"Will you be coming back here, Cath', or what?" Jill asked through her tears.

"I don't think so, Jill. The memories are just too fierce here for me to come back. I thought I'd always go on with Joe, but that's not meant to be, I guess, so there's no sense in my holding on to it, now is there." Cathy had really begun to hate her other false 'friend' and what it was doing to her self-esteem, and was suddenly astutely observant and cynical; the listlessness and apathy in her voice tore into Jill's heart.

"I've tried to hold onto it for over a year and it's almost broken me in two, so...." A wave of her hands, a shattering sigh that ended on the sounds of an almost sob. "'Bye, Jill, have a good life, and that officer is somewhere out there for you. You'll find him, I just know it."

She hugged Jill tightly. They kissed each other on the cheek, and Cathy turned to step into the cab that would take her to the bus depot. She had refused Jill's plea to drive her to the station; Remembering another heartrending goodbye at another time, Cathy now understood, and didn't want a lingering goodbye from her friend either. This way, she stepped into the taxicab and was gone.

CHAPTER TEN

Cathy was very sick when she had arrived, and knew, without even thinking about it, in her mothers' house her friend, the bottle, would not be tolerated. She had slowly started withdrawal from it right after she had given notice at the hospital. Before she left the Springs on the thirty-hour bus trip, she knew the bottle had to go, and the last one was deposited with a derisive grin of contempt into the garbage bag.

She was getting very tired of this false companionship anyway, and all she had needed was the positive incentive to get it out of her life. Leaving a job she loved was a very difficult thing and Dr Anderson had promised her a good reference for when she was ready to restart working. But she felt that would take some time to do.

Her mom was so glad to see her home again, but was very concerned at her pallid complexion and lack of strength, and it was soon obvious to her that Cathy was very ill.

The very next morning she called the family doctor to come see Cathy because of the severe nausea, fever, and wracking abdominal pain she was suffering.

While Dr Sutton was examining her, Cathy asked, "Mom, would you please make some tea? That sounds so good." And when she had gone from the room, Cathy confided the cause of her sickness to the concerned doctor, her long abuse of alcohol.

"Please, give me something for the nausea, and don't tell Mom. As far as she knows I caught something on the bus trip home, flu, or something. Please, doctor!" she beseeched him.

Dr Sutton told her in a firm and no-nonsense voice, "All right, Cathy, we'll try some medication for twenty-four hours, but if I see you're becoming more dehydrated and your fever isn't going down, you're going to the hospital for intravenous feeding, and I'll take no guff about it, okay?"

Cathy pulled through the ultimatum the good doctor had given her, and that night, finally, began to keep fluids down.

Almost every hour on the hour throughout the next day her mom brought her something: tea, broth, fruit juice, hot water with a pinch of salt, and little by little it began to seep back into her system and stay there. She forced herself to swallow whatever was brought her and when the doctor came back that afternoon after office hours, he was pleased the fever was coming down, the nausea beginning to let up.

Cathy had been neglecting her health in every way ever since the bottle had come into the picture, and it was a long, painful, sickening time of recuperation.

For the next week-and-a-half, she regained her strength with her mom prodding her to eat more. "Eat some of this baked chicken, honey, I'll get you another piece," she would urge, or, "Have another slice of this roast beef, and some more green beans, they're good for you," and always refilling the water pitcher beside the bed; always, "'happen to have' this Jell-O with fruit ready to eat and it'll spoil if not eaten soon."

Bleary-eyed and weak, Cathy finally managed to get up and sit in the rocker beside the bed long enough for her mother to flutter around her changing the sheets, fluffing the pillows, and clucking her soft voice to her with incidental news of the day.

In two months, her devil beginning to be behind her, she had been ready and willing to work in the garden, mow the lawn, trim the hedges, and do things that needed to be done around the house. The busyness and fresh air cleared the cobwebs from her mind and wearied her body enough to be able to sleep at night, at least for most of it. She still buried her head into the pillow and sobbed her heartache, but it wasn't the totally depressive or soul-consuming way it used to be.

She was learning to cope with it, learning to live without Joe in her life. She hadn't been able to talk to her mom about Joe, or talk to anyone about him. It was buried too deep to frame words and try to verbalize, or to formulate a sentence to express her thoughts and feeling. It was still too final, too close, too... hard.

"Mom," Cathy stated on Monday morning at the breakfast table, "I'm going into town and see if there are any jobs open at the hospital. Might as well put my application in; I can't live off you forever. It's been great, but maybe I better see about getting back to work again. Do you want to go along for any shopping or anything?"

"No, dear, you go ahead. The car will probably need gas. Do you have enough cash for that and the trip?"

"Yeh, mom, I still have a little cash I brought with me, so I'm fine," she returned. "I'll open an account at the bank later when I get a job, then I can start paying you back a little financially for all the food and stuff you've bought for me."

"That's okay, honey, don't worry 'bout that," she responded warmly.

Arriving at St Francis Hospital, she found her way to the third floor employment office, and requested an application form.

When the clerk inquired as to what position she was applying for, Cathy told her, "I don't know, anything that would give me employment. Nurses' aide would be good."

She filled out the form and handed it back to the clerk.

When she saw Cathy had had over a year of training in x-ray she called her supervisor, Sister Dominica.

Sr Dominica was a tall, gentle-looking personage with wire-rimmed glasses perched on a pert and small nose. Her half-formed smile and blue eyes were surrounded by soft wrinkly crinkles that pushed up against the white starched coif that framed her face, and her voice when she spoke was soft, but with a no-foolishness, businesslike tone.

"I see, Miss Cabal," she started, "you have almost fifteen months of x-ray technology training. Why did you leave it and not finish?"

"I became very seriously ill, Sister," Cathy rejoined, "and had to come home. I've been home for three months and just now getting my health back and need to return to work."

"Would you want to resume your training? It would be shameful to waste the time you've already put into it if it's something you want to pursue," her voice gently suggested.

"I'd like to continue in x-ray, but I can't afford to pay for schooling. There I was paid a stipend for working, and learning at the same time, plus I was taking call at two dollars per night extra, rotating every third week with the other two tech's."

"Well, we have a similar program here and before we even talk anymore let me take you to meet Dr Vogel, our chief radiologist, and see what he has to say. He might be encouraged to have you finish your training and, well... let's go see him first," she ended with a smile.

Cathy was introduced to a medium height, slightly rotund man with a graying flattop haircut; dark-rimmed glasses pushed up against his rounded cheeks, giving him a very elfish appearance.

To enhance the effect, he was wearing dark green slacks and a bright yellow shirt. His smile behind the pencil-thin moustache that lined his upper lip was quick and abrupt, and completed the illusion.

Dr Vogel turned from dictating the report of the x-ray study he was reading and leaned back in the swivel chair, eyeing Cathy in a casual manner. Sr Dominica told him what had been talked about, and asked him to talk to Cathy. She left the room, telling Cathy to return to the employment office when she was finished.

With his hands locked behind his head and leaning back in his swivel chair, he asked, "What kind of illness took you down, Miss Cabal?"

"I have to be honest, doctor. I'm coming off alcohol addiction of over a year duration. I'm over it now, have been dry for three months, and need to get back to work and get my life involved again."

She spoke lightly, sat square and relaxed, and looked him in the eyes, not defiantly, but as honestly as she could. "No one at home knows this, not even my Mom whom I've been staying with. The reason for the addiction is gone and won't be reoccurring because it's over. I've had no desire for alcohol these past months, no regrets that I'm done with it."

He looked at her long and thoughtfully. "Would you be willing to go to a couple of Alcoholic Anonymous meetings, for my peace of mind, and to reassure yourself that what you say is so, not just wishful thinking?"

"Yes, if that's what you recommend," she returned without hesitation. She admitted finally, with an internal sigh, this is what she had hoped for, too.

"Good. We have a similar training program like you had there, pays eighty dollars a month which includes call pay, and we are short-staffed right now. I'd like to get your records from Memorial Hospital. Give me a week, and I'll call you and let you know."

He turned to his view-box panels to continue with his reports, "Oh, and by the way," he turned back, as in an afterthought, "I'd like to be your sponsor at your AA meetings if that's all right with you. See, I've been there, too, and if this works out, we'll both come out ahead. And no one needs to know anything right now. I'll keep it confidential."

It worked out very well, indeed, for over the next year Cathy worked as if her life depended on it. She attended the AA meetings every week for the first three months of her internship, with Dr Vogel being there for most of them.

Then gradually, she began to phase herself out of the program, knowing deep inside she was going to be all right.

The loneliness was dispelled by the friends she made quickly, and the doctoral interns who came on to her strongly—and one very compellingly—was very flattering to her ego even though she turned them all down.

She took her National Board Examination in the Spring of the following year, passed it with flying colors, and earned the title of American Registered X-ray Technician. She bought the "ARXT" pin that was her badge of honor and placed it on the left upper chest of her uniform with, and just above, the new name label that proudly stated:

Cathy Cabal
Registered X-Ray Technician

• • •

The next four years passed swiftly, and Cathy worked her way to the top managerial position of Chief X-Ray Technician. The presiding Chief Tech, Pat Dunne, who had been there for many years, decided to retire and Cathy spent all of her time now in administrative duties. She began to miss the day to day involvement with patient's, the active participation in their initial exams and beginning road to recovery, but reveled in the challenge of blending the world of management to the world of the working technician.

Sometimes, though, the challenges could be tiring and oh, so very nerve-wracking. The push was on from top echelon management for less overhead and fewer man-hours, and at the same time cover more work areas.

She was sitting at her office desk and wearily reading reports—always reading something—late one evening when there was a knock on her office door.

"Cathy, may I come in?"

"Sure, Dr Sazama, come on in. You can interrupt this droll reading any time. What can I do for you?" She lay her reading material aside. Dr 'S' was a favorite friend whom she had met when she first started as a trainee. He had helped her on numerous occasions through the years.

"Well," he breezily looked around, "as you've probably heard we're opening a new x-ray clinic in the medical building in Far Hills, and when it's done I'm going to need someone to help set the office up and get it into operation. Do you know of anyone who would be at all interested? Or would you..." he paused, "...consider the position?"

He had seated himself in the chair across from Cathy's desk, pulled it closer, put his elbows on her desk with his head cupped in his hands and looked very earnestly at her.

"You'd be in control of the whole shebang, and would be in charge of hiring, books, quality control, reports, appointments... everything. I know you've been here awhile, and probably have good benefits, andsoforth, but I really need someone who knows what the heck they're doing. If you won't consider it for yourself, perhaps you'd know of someone who'd be capable to handle this? We're hoping to have it ready in about three months' time."

He let his breath out in a long sigh, and looked at her, his head tilted slightly still cupped in his hands, his eyes bright with expectance and hope. He focused directly on her surprised expression.

"Whoa, Dr 'S', you've taken me by complete surprise. Are you asking if I would be interested in your offer?"

The doctor shook his head affirmatively, and Cathy took a long thoughtful time following his proposal before she started with the questions.

Taking in a deep breath, she proceeded to ask, "How many people will be manning the clinic?"

"Three, and you... Monday through Friday."

"Monday through Friday you say...nice. Benefits?"

"Almost will match the hospital after six months. Two radiologists, new building, sick leave days, vacation time, and in full charge andsoforth."

"You are tempting me very much, doctor," she exclaimed after their discussion. "But please let me think about this, and if I decide against it I'll come up with some names for you. Is that okay?"

Having agreed to meet in three days to seal the offer one way or another, Dr 'S' exited whistling a jaunty tune.

Shaking her head and with a little smile, Cathy decided she had had enough of reports and mental struggle for the day and went home to her apartment. Thinking about the offer meant she could stay in this apartment, too. She wouldn't have to move again, a thought that brought a feeling of dread to the pit of her stomach; she hated any thought of moving and really didn't want to leave her neat beautiful apartment, a point that swayed in favor of the new proposition.

Reasoning out loud to herself and to Boots, her small black and white terrier dog, "I could get a little more 'hands on' with the patient's again, be involved with their care. I've certainly been away from that. The pressure cooker is on now from the top for faster patient put-through, less time with them and faster turnover. Cut... cut... cut," as she snipped her fingers through the air, "everything, including compassionate time with the ones who need it. Where are the patient's going to get the TLC they require if everyone down the line treats them like a... a... wood box that has to be checked off quickly?"

She picked Boots up and nuzzled his happy face. "Time-control studies, renovating the department to cut wasteful nooks and crannies, more powerful equipment, new procedures. I suppose it's all good, and a peek at the computer age that's coming. What do you think, Boots?" Her tirade ended in a deep sigh as Boots kissed her face. Then another thought hit her, "Do I want to spend the rest of my career just managing it from an office and passing by the door of the procedures room? Nope! I really believe I want to do it!" She laughed, "I want to go in that door."

With that last confirmation of what she'd unconsciously felt deep within her, she knew her mind was made up, and she would be taking Dr Sazama's offer.

"Well, Boots, I'm back in uniform again," she giggled.

The month-long notice she gave the hospital was a very long and apprehensive time. Everywhere she looked, she could see something in which she had had a hand in developing and at times she had many doubts about her decision. When she was at home and away from there, she focused more completely on the coming phase of her profession at the new medical clinic and her confidence expanded more with each passing day.

Her replacement was already hired from within the department and being trained, and she knew he was going to be a good fit for the department.

Dr Sazama had told her nothing about the other radiologist and she was curious about him. The only thing she knew was that he was coming from the West Coast and joining Dr Sazama's practice after ten years of service in the Marine Corps.

His arrival one month before the opening of the complex was unsettling to Cathy. He appeared to be quiet, about six-foot three, with dark wavy hair; a lean and muscular man with gray eyes that seemed to be able to look deep into an x-ray study... or anyone.

She felt an attraction to him that unnerved her, the first such feeling she could honestly say since Joe, and she was totally confused and somewhat shaken. When she was introduced to him that day by John Sazama, she felt the tension between them immediately. She shook her finger in disapproval at herself, and reminded herself again, for the millionth time, that she didn't have room for such feelings, or time.

Getting the clinic set up with all the myriad details that had to be taken care of was her first priority. Hiring of personnel; setting up the appointment schedule; consultation on the finishing of the rooms and placement of equipment; conferring with the accountant; office decor...; the list went on forever.

And Dr Evan Mitchell and all his influential personality had to wait until she had time to deal with it.

Eventually, the clinic, with only a few mishaps, was open for business. Their clientele were referrals by the surrounding area physicians whose patients preferred a more personal setting for their exams other than the hospital. The medical center was prepared to do most any kind of exam except those which required highly specialized equipment. Examinations and scans requiring intravenous injection of material to show arteries, veins, or the heart were better left to the larger departments.

Ultrasound was brought in with a technician trained in its use, and Cathy found this, particularly, to be a fascinating new development in diagnostic availability. Watching the movements of a growing baby in the mothers' womb, seeing stones in the gallbladder, tumors or cysts in the liver, pancreas, or kidney, was an experience Cathy never dreamt about, and she eagerly learned as much about the procedure as she could.

The personnel filled her in on 'their' Doctor Mitchell. He was a widower; his wife and baby daughter had died in a car accident when struck by a drunk driver; he was thirty-one years old, owned a couple of horses, and other animals, and loved to ride.

He was buying a house in the country and had rented an apartment, by the month, close to the clinic. They wondered if he left the Marines because his wife and child were gone.

The girls raved about his niceness, his gentlemanly consideration of them, and two of the three girls knew that they loved this man, and would marry him 'in an instant' if he would have them.

Dr Sazama was already married, the father of a teenage daughter and college-bound son, too much of a father figure for them to even think about him that way. But Dr Evan Mitchell was a different matter; he needed the compassionate tender mercies of the technicians, if each had her way.

Cathy was coolly polite to him, very professional, very aloof, very careful in what she said and did around him.

The weather was cooling again, and barbecue's were beginning to ebb as Summer started to transform into a beautiful Fall. Cathy decided to throw a last big barbeque in her apartment backyard, and invited everyone in the department for the informal get-together party with Wendy, Katie, Rose, and their dates, Dr 'S' and wife, and Dr Mitchell and a date if he wanted.

It was set for the last Saturday late afternoon of September and guests began arriving at five o'clock. The card tables were set up outside, the charcoal briquettes were beginning to glow in the grill, soft drinks of all description were set into coolers of ice, the snacks were put out in their colorful containers, and all was ready.

Cathy had changed into a bright red pullover shirt and gray slacks with a red band around her hair that pulled it off her face but let it hang long and loose in the back. Bright red sandals adorned her feet. She bounced around the tables and chairs, straightened, covered bowls against flies, checked the coals. When the group had settled in, she brought out the tender steaks she was planning to grill, still soaking in her favorite marinade.

It didn't take long for them to devour the eats, almost empty the cooler of drinks, then sit back contentedly groaning their 'have-eaten-too-much-but-everything-was-so-good-couldn't-stop' syndrome of happy misery.

Cathy was delighted her party had been such a great success, but wondered why Evan Mitchell had not brought a date.

She had heard through the clinic grapevine that he was supposedly already seeing someone, and her curiosity was biting at her to ask, but her aloof coolness wouldn't let her. She didn't want him to think she cared one way or the other. And did she?

After everyone had eaten and snacked their utmost, lawn games had been played and put way again, and the darkness had been with them for awhile, Dr Sazama and wife started to say their goodnight and thanks to Cathy for having them. The party broke up rather quickly after that, but Evan Mitchell volunteered to stay and help with the cleanup.

"It's okay, Cathy. It's early enough yet and I don't have anything else to do. I'd really like to help," he volunteered. "It won't take near as long to put all this away with an extra pair of hands."

He helped carry the tables and chairs to the storeroom, the empty bowls inside, emptied the coolers of their icy particles and dried them. When he had finished this, Cathy was just cleaning up the last dish and wiping everything down.

"See, I told you it wouldn't take as long," he kidded. "Anything else need doing?"

"No, that does it and thanks a lot. I appreciate it," she returned.

Even though she was grateful for his help, she still kept away from him, mentally and purposely blocking out his charm and boyish smile that had a tendency to almost disarm her.

"Umm, Cathy, I'm going to go to the country tomorrow to exercise my horses. I have two and need a rider for Bitsy. She's really a sweet gentle little horse. Would you like to go with me?" He added hastily, "Unless, of course, you're busy or something. I know it's kind-of a last minute invitation, but I think you'd enjoy it, fresh country air and everything."

She was tempted. She loved animals, and riding horses. She remembered when she and... "No, I'm sorry, but I'm afraid I'm busy tomorrow," she lied tersely, her face draining of color at the thought of Joe.

"All right, maybe some other time then." The look of puzzled disappointment that clouded his face lasted but a moment when seeing her face change and her eyes suddenly squint up, "I'll see you at work Monday then. Goodnight, Cathy, and thanks for tonight."

He was out the door and gone in just a few strides of his long legs.

It wasn't until Monday morning that word was put around that the woman Dr Mitchell 'was seeing' was his sister. He had decided to come here and join Dr Sazama in his practice because his sister lived nearby, and it had been a long time since he had had a chance to be with her and could watch her and her husbands' kids grow up; they had three, and also wanted their uncle to be an active participant in their growing years. The sister, Judy, and Ken, knew how he had suffered after the loss of his own family, and was delighted that he had decided to move so close to home.

Why did Cathy feel such relief? What did it matter to her who the woman in Evan Mitchell's life was? But somehow, she did feel relieved there was no other 'woman', and then terribly guilty at feeling that way. She believed—no, knew! she wanted nothing to do with him, so why should she begrudge him a life? Or was a hint of jealousy creeping into her? No, she had never felt jealousy or envy in her life, only loneliness lately. A lot of that.

The weeks rolled by, and all of them were busy with settling into their routine. Getting the scheduled examinations running smoothly in each of the two x-ray rooms, the reports typed and out to the physicians, the accounting books ready for the CPA, and all the dozens of details that needed to be done each day kept Cathy very busy, sometimes way past the closing hour of five o'clock.

Dr Mitchell had stayed some of these nights, dictating exams and consulting with radiologists in the hospital by phone, getting reports on patient's that had needed extra follow up work done.

It was on one of these late seven o'clock nights that he and Cathy ended up their chores at about the same time.

"Cathy, you're working so late so many nights, and the company can't pay you for all you've been doing. It's late, I'm tired and hungry, and I believe you are tired and hungry also. May I buy your dinner? We could go to Uncle Al's restaurant for some chicken, or fish, or whatever you want. Or wherever you want. All I know is that I want to get out of here, and I'm sure you do, too. How 'bout it?" He looked up from his swivel chair, and tiredly ran his fingers through his hair. His starched white lab coat was wrinkled and wilted from the days' work, and he stood up and pulled it off throwing it into the hamper in his office closet. Picking a gray silk scarf from the shelf, he draped it around his neck, pulled a fingertip-length dark bluewool coat off the hanger, hunched into it and buttoned it almost all the way to the top.

It was snowing and windy, and peeking through the blinds at the cold blustery weather outside, he also grabbed a blue wool hat from the closet shelf and planted it on his dark hair.

Wearily Cathy let her defenses down long enough to value the offer and decided to accept it. She was too hungry also, to want to take the time to fix something at home.

"Thank you, doctor, I appreciate this, but would you mind if we stop by my apartment so I can throw something into Boots dish? It's right on the way to Uncle Al's and won't take but a minute. Usually, I'd be home by now, feeding him while making my own, but I wouldn't enjoy my dinner knowing he's getting pretty hungry. I don't leave anything out for him to eat, just a water dish."

He helped her on with her red cashmere coat, and Cathy retrieved her purse from the desk drawer. They walked to the door, and pulled it closed behind them, locked it and was on their way.

CHAPTER ELEVEN

That night started a different relationship between Cathy and Mitch. They talked late and long that evening, mainly about his country home and the renovation he was going to have to do, and his love for his horses, Ranger and Bitsy, and his other animals. He had her laughing with stories of what stunts the animals had pulled, "All without training and in total innocence," he recalled to her.

She listened, and was strangely relaxed being with him, feeling curiously sheltered and comfortable.

She could not retain her cool indifference at work anymore. She had seen a very vulnerable side to Dr Mitchell; a still, quiet nature to his personality that was very appealing to her. His eyes and face lit up when he spoke of his animals, and then clouded over when he 'just knew that Bernadette and my baby, Marcia, would have loved it, and would have grown up with an appreciation of the life on our ranch'. The mention was very brief and torturous for him, and Cathy could see the pain in his eyes. It had been almost two years since they were gone, and the sharp edge of jagged loneliness could be read into his behavior, his need to confide to someone about his plans and his dreams, especially for the ranch.

•   •   •

"Cathy, what do you think about this color? The decorator wants to put it in the living area, and I keep telling her... no, I want a sunny cream color, not this... this whatever it is color. What do you think, does this look like cream? I'm not too good with colors." He lifted the paint can closer to her so she could see it better. He was dissatisfied with the shade and frustrated, and didn't know what to tell the decorator.

"To me, that looks like... well, I won't say it, but definitely not a sunny cream in my estimation. Tell her to add a lot of white to this and a hint of red to soften it. No," she changed her mind and shook her head, "better yet, start over with another base color," she advised him, "this one is too muddied already."

Little by little, he had been seeking her advice on different things; style combinations, drapery materials and designs, colors....

He shoved a picture under her nose, "Cathy, would this rug look all right under the dining room table and chairs?"

He always liked and agreed with her opinion and what she told him about the subject in question, yet he had not invited her back out to the house.

He told her, "Oh, my, it's in such a mess, but someday soon, when it's a little further along, I most assuredly would love for you to see it."

• • •

A thick snow was falling, and the world had suddenly turned into a wonderland of soft, muted sounds, the white, bright stillness transfixing the raw edges of her harried nerves to a calmness that Cathy had not felt for awhile.

Christmas season was upon them and shopping was a priority after working hours. Even though it seemed harder to commute in the snow, everything else was accordingly slowed down, and even just that much change in the pace seemed to help transform her stress to a more gentle amble as she roamed the stores.

She found a beautiful, quilted, rose-colored bathrobe with satin lapels for her Mom with slippers that matched; leather jackets and gloves for her two brothers, and she hoped the sizes were right. With these acquisitions done, her thoughts then turned to the clinic and her personnel.

Definitely leather-trimmed/daily notation/desk calendar/pen and pencil sets for each of the two doctors, one in dark brown and the other in light brown; and for Wendy, a framed painting she had admired at the art store a couple of weeks ago; a beautiful crystal vase with an etched design on it for Katie, who was always receiving gorgeous bouquets from admirers; and a porcelain figurine set of a Romeo singing to his sweetheart for Rose, the one who loved romantic things such as this.

It had taken a couple weeks of after-work searching to find these treasures, and an entire evening wrapping them in the colorful, shiny papers and ribbons from which Cathy loved to make a creation.

She was working on the living room floor—big mistake—as Boots was 'helping' her by growling at and tangling himself up in the ribbons, paper, and clutter of tape, scissors, and paraphernalia that she required to produce a beautiful package.

"Come, on Boots, don't help me, okay?" was her constant rejoinder to him as she smilingly, once again, rescued and retrieved yet another roll of red ribbon from his playful attacks.

Dr Mitchell hurriedly confided between patient exams, "Cathy, I'm having a Christmas party at my house week from next Saturday night. It's kind-of a party and housewarming combined. It's finally put together good enough to have people over, even going to put a Christmas tree and decorations up. It's not done yet, by any means, as the entire main level and only one bedroom upstairs is finished. I hope you'll come see what you've helped me with. Will you?" he asked. "Hopefully, everyone from the office can make it. My sis and family are coming also. Six o'clock for cocktails, and I'll have a buffet set up with plenty of food. A friend of mine that I used to go to school with is a caterer and he's going all out for me for this party."

"You'll have to give me directions on how to get there, Mitch, and, yes, I'd love to come. I'm very anxious to see what you've done," she replied.

At his suggestion, it was decided between all of them to make this party the office party as well, so as to not take away time from some who had to go distances to get to their families.

The gala was set for Saturday, the twenty-second, just days before Christmas Day, and they would then reopen for business on Wednesday the twenty-sixth, giving everyone a few days breather.

Cathy was the first to arrive. The snow was piled quite high against the fence surrounding the massive yard, but she pulled as far up as she could in the cleared driveway area.

Sitting there a moment enjoying the vista, she looked around her, then gathered the gifts in a large basket and proceeded up the cleared walkway onto the steps of the porch. The porch ran across the entire front of the house, then turned and disappeared around the left side toward the back. At the corner were some bushes leaning with their weight of heavy snow against the outer railing.

She proceeded across the gray boards and rang the bell.

When he opened the right side of the large double doors, she stepped onto an expansive foyer with light oak flooring in a mosaic design. Her eyes fell immediately downward.

When he noticed her admiring gaze, he said with pride, "All it had needed was a refinishing and waxing to bring out its original luster."

She slipped out of her boots, placed them in the rubber boot caddy sitting alongside the door to catch the drips, then glanced up to a small chandelier which hung in the middle of the foyer. Tied to it was a miniature bundle of real mistletoe.

As she handed him her coat and scarf, she looked at the staircase where it started slightly to the right and marched up along the wall, than curved itself against the back wall to open up onto what seemed to be a wide hallway upstairs. The entire dark banister railing—Is that walnut? she wondered—was draped in a long thick rope of greenery, with large red bows and a few clusters of small silver and gold balls threaded among the woven branches.

It was a very striking picture against the white turned spokes and dark stair-treads on the steps. Cathy was amazed at the decorating that he and his caterer friend and wife had accomplished.

On the right side of the foyer and through a large arched doorway stood a tall pine tree in a much higher ceilinged room.

He told her, "That's the music alcove."

The tree was highlighted stunningly by the set of three floor to ceiling bay windows behind it that jutted out from the room and gave the tree its background. It was very simply decorated with a few strands of miniature white lights, with tiny white doves, red cardinals, and bluebirds scattered among the branches. Only a few small glittering bells of all different colors gave it added sparkle.

Mitch explained with delight the beautiful wreath on the tip-top of the tree. "Greenery cut from the bottom of the tree is intertwined around a stretched-out coat hanger and the hanger then tied onto the treetop. Tiny blue lights are braided among the cuttings, and that's angel hair draped and surrounding the entire wreath. The effect really gives it a dramatic, yet very soft celestial feeling, don't you think?"

He then led her to the left of the foyer and through a swinging door to the L-shaped kitchen. At the end of the long side was the dining room which stretched out towards the back of the house. The living room abutted to this room with a great arching doorway between to hint of the separation between them, and it stretched out along the back of the house. A fireplace, with a roaring fire dancing, dominated the back wall of this room. A feast was set on a long table to the right of the fireplace, and the music alcove in which the tree was spotlighted blended very beautifully into this living space. On the interior wall across the room nestled a built-in bar, the firelight dancing and sparkling on the crystalware put there for the celebration.

Subtle gold carpeting was on the living room and music room floors, and the dining area had a beautiful light oak floor onto which Mitch had thrown a colorful Navajo-style area rug under the oak table and chairs.

The decorator did come up with a pretty cream color, Cathy noticed, and it gives a warm, pleasant feeling to this room.

There were no pictures on the walls, but a few sprays of greenery with shiny red balls were tacked here and there to take away the bareness, and they seemed totally in place. A few borrowed chairs and snack tables were scattered around the rooms.

The party was a spirited success and everyone was totally impressed with the work he had done in such a short time. He had brought out pictures and shown the 'before I started state of disrepair' he had encountered. "The roof and chimney's have been repaired, but the outside of the house will have to wait until warmer weather."

"Silent Night, Holy Night..."

The singing of Christmas carols later in the evening around the firelight was emotionally draining for Cathy, and glancing over to Mitch, she saw tears welling in his eyes.

She berated herself. Oh, great, Cabal, how selfish can you be? Compared to what he's lost, and how recent, you have a nerve feeling sorry for yourself!

It was about that same moment Dr Sazama and his wife made motions of getting ready to reluctantly leave. It was already past midnight. She couldn't believe it. Where did the time go tonight? Mitch's sister and family had left around ten to put the children to bed.

They were soon all out the door, and Cathy decided to repay the favor owed to Mitch by helping him clean up, as he had helped her seemingly eons ago. Everyone had assisted earlier by taking trays, dishes, glasses, and anything else to the kitchen; all that was needed was to wash them and put everything away, and this undertaking did not require a long time.

She called to him in the living room, "Mitch, where does this silver tray go?"

"Alongside the sink in that narrow cabinet, I think, Cathy," he sang back as he walked back into the kitchen.

"Well, I guess that does it." She looked around the kitchen while drying her hands, then hung the towel up on the refrigerator door handle. "Are you spending tomorrow with Judy and the family?"

"Just Christmas Day. I'm going to do some work around here I want to get at. Odds and ends things I need to putter with. I have the one bedroom done upstairs, as I've said, but I need to sit down and think about what needs to be done in the other two, and the baths. Had no trouble with the lavatory down here, but want to do something special up there, and don't know what yet. Thanks, Cath', for staying and helping put all this down. Couldn't have done it without you."

"Yeah, you could've, just would've taken longer," she jested back to him.

"How 'bout you? Are you going to your Mother's for the holidays?"

"Only on Christmas Day also. Going to take a couple of R and R days and just do nothing... I think, I don't know. I may get bored out of my mind with nothing to do," she said.

He gathered her coat from the guest closet under the stairwell, then helped her put it on.

The aroma of the pine tree wafted into the room, and taking a deep breath of it, Cathy held it in her lungs, tilting her face up with eyes closed to embrace it and savor it.

It was a startling sensation when she felt the kiss on her lips. Opening her eyes wide in complete surprise, she let her breath out in a muffled poof of air. Mitch was facing her, and with his smiling eyes beckoned her to look up at the chandelier.

They were standing directly under the mistletoe.

He grinned openly at her, "Couldn't resist the temptation. You looked so... kissable... right then."

The smile faded, "And you still do." With those words he put his hands on her shoulders, pulled her to him and kissed her again, a longer, very soulful, urgent kiss that rocked Cathy to her toes.

"Please, Mitch...," Cathy tried to talk. Her senses were reeling, her heart started doing flip-flops.

"Okay, Cathy, sorry if I took unfair advantage. But," his eyes started twinkling and a roguish grin again twitched at his mouth, "we are under the mistletoe, and this is fairyland this time of year, isn't it?" he questioned breathlessly.

She had to laugh in spite of the quaking feeling that had invaded her as she stepped away and began to frantically pull on her boots. "Yes, it definitely is fairyland, all right. I better get going. It's getting very late. Thanks for the party tonight. It was fun." And she turned, walked through the door he held open and headed toward the car.

The roads were cleared. The snow was luminous where the bright moon glanced across it. She had a lot to think about and she drove slowly, and as she wound her way along the country road she began to think how it was like driving in a picture postcard.

The trees were heavy with their white burden, and the fence posts along the road looked sterilized by the pureness of the snow gathered against them. The farmhouse roofs seemed to somehow shimmer in the moonlight, the house shapes and outlines in stark contrast to the brightness around them.

She tried very hard not to think about what had happened.

It had been seven years since anyone had—anyone, period—had kissed her. Was that the reason it seemed so special? No, there has been a feeling between myself and Dr Evan Mitchell ever since we met, she had to admit that much. Where do I want this to go? Do I want it to go anywhere?

The peacefulness of the country scene helped her to untangle herself, really helped her to let her guard down, and she pulled to the side of the road on the crest of a hill and stared at the rolling fields and panorama that unfolded before her in the moonlight.

There was no living thing moving within her vision, and all of a sudden it seemed to be echoing her life. There was no one special moving there either, and the weight of loneliness suddenly squeezed the tears from her. She sat there for a time and cried; cried for the past that was never to be; cried for the emotions Mitch had brought to the surface and which she thought she had put down forever. She sat for a long time.

Shivering in the beginning cold with the car turned off, she restarted it and drove on home. Boots welcomed her with a sleepy yawn then crawled back into his nice warm blanketed wicker basket.

When the phone rang he yelped as usual, and she jumped.

"Who on earth is calling me at this hour?" Her heart started to beat in a rapid frantic rhythm when she thought, Oh, God... Mom! And with the beat now hammering in her throat she choked out, "Hello."

"Oh, good, you made it. I was starting to get worried about you getting home. I've been calling for twenty minutes and I was about to send out the Mounties looking for you."

It was Mitch and the concern in his voice was genuine, "I hated seeing you drive alone at this time of night."

She hefted a big sigh of relief, "Oh, Mitch, how nice of you to check on me. I stopped and looked at the beautiful scenery along the road. The full moon seems to have made it a wonderland out there. You live in nice country, Mitch."

Her heart still raced, and now the hand holding the phone suddenly started shaking, and the tremor in her voice was not missed by Mitch.

"Are you all right, Cathy? You seem upset. I hope the telephone ringing at this time of morning didn't scare you."

"No, I'm fine, just tired, I guess."

Mitch said excitedly, "If you get bored tomorrow, come on out and we'll take a ride in the sleigh I found in the barn a couple days ago. It might be fun to see if I can get Ranger to pull it. He's a pretty good ole' boy, smart, and adjusts very quickly. He's not too edgy for a thoroughbred. How 'bout it? Would you keep it in mind?" With barely a pause for breath, he continued, "Well, since you're home and tired, I'll let you hit the sack. 'Night, Cathy. Call me if you want to come out." And before she could answer, he had hung up.

She slept later than usual the next morning. Boots was dancing at the door wanting out when she awakened. She struggled out of bed, and grudgingly and still only half-awake, opened the door. "Go at it, Boots," when she finally let him relieve himself.

When she had showered and dressed, and had her breakfast, she sat wondering, now what?

Many projects around the house didn't seem to have any appeal to her. Cleaning cupboards, or cleaning closets just didn't seem to be the things she wanted to do.

She was edgy, nervous, couldn't seem to sit still, the voice on the telephone in the wee hours of this morning kept permeating her confused thoughts. The party; the kiss; the mixed-up feelings she had when she was with him kept intruding in her thoughts.

"Might as well give in to it, Boots, and go on out there if he really meant his invitation." She picked up the phone and called him.

He laughed excitedly, "I was hoping you would come. I have the sleigh all cleaned up, found all the harness work, and was just thinking about putting Ranger into it. Come on out and bring Boots along—he should have some fun, too. I'll wait until you get here to try Ranger. This should be great. Wear warm things."

When she arrived, he met her at the car and led her to the barn where the sleigh, Ranger and Bitsy were. The barn was warm, and smelled of an almost forgotten odor of hay and animals. She liked it; it reminded her of when she was a child growing up on the farm.

"I don't know what Ranger is going to think about all this," Mitch whispered almost conspiratorially to her as he lifted the harness onto Ranger's back. Ranger snorted and eyed Mitch, and Cathy could almost decipher Ranger's movements as asking Mitch, "What the heck are you doing?"

"Do you think he'll do it, Mitch?" she whispered back, as though they were accomplices in a deed that Ranger was not to overhear even as they were standing right beside him.

But, their efforts were to no avail, the harness was much too small for Ranger. It was an old harness, and evidently the horses, in the era of the use of the sleigh were much smaller animals, and the adjustments would not let out enough to go around Ranger's ample girth.

"Well, ole' boy, you're off the hook. I didn't even think about the size of the harness as being too small. I guess we'll have to postpone our ride." Mitch was disappointed, and slightly chagrined to have forgotten to check on that detail.

Boots was having a ball; all the myriads of different smells and scents for him to check out! He made them laugh when he came up against his first young kitten, a tiny gray fur-ball with a soft squeaky mew. It had gotten adventurous and wandered too far from its mother and tried to cuddle up with Boots for warmth and security.

Boots sniffed and tentatively licked on it, and the puffball kitten instinctively tried to crawl under him. Boots was having none of that, however, and came wagging a begging tail to Cathy to, "Do something about that little thing, please," the wagging seemed to say.

Mitch pushed hay down from the loft for the horses, and, still laughing, Cathy picked up Boots and all headed for the house. The aroma of the pine tree hit them when they walked in, and she had to catch up with Boots before he could do any mischief at it; confining him to the kitchen was the only thing.

They then strolled into the music room to admire the pine tree.

She contemplated, Ah, yes, was it only last night, and am I out of my mind to have come here? Am I really ready for a relationship with this tall, handsome doctor? And he was one who would not settle for less than a meaningful relationship; would not take the chance of hurting her, or being hurt, with an affair, she felt this without question. She could sense how much he ached, and knew from her own pain of loss that she could not settle for less either.

He stoked the fireplace, placing another log onto it. "How about some hot chocolate, Cathy, and maybe something to eat? Have a lot of stuff left over from last night and it'll go to waste if not eaten soon." He spoke gentle and warm, interrupting her thoughts.

Could he be remembering also?

She sighed, and he reached over, took her hand and led her to the kitchen. She fixed the sandwiches from the roast beef with all the trimmings as he conjured up the hot chocolate. They then dished out potato salad, gelatin salad, and whatever struck their fancy.

As they were eating, he leaned over once with a napkin in his hand and wiped a dab of horseradish from Cathy's upper lip, then leaned across the small table and kissed her very lightly alongside that lip.

He smiled at her, his breath quickening, "You do look good enough to eat, Cathy."

He continued to munch his sandwich, his gray eyes now smoldering and smoky with his restrained feelings.

Cathy put her sandwich aside for a moment to sip the creamy chocolate and glanced up at him. He had a devilish smile on his face again and was starting to reach across with his napkin. She almost let him wipe the moustache of chocolate off, but quickly brought her hand up and covered her mouth, her heart racing, her body shaking.

They talked, bantered back and forth and wore away the rest of the afternoon. He finally brought out the floor plans he had been experimenting with for the upstairs rooms.

"See, I want to do something special in the Master bedroom, but not exactly sure what I want yet. Can you give me any ideas? What would a woman like for convenience, closet space, lighting... and anything else?"

She felt he was specifically asking her what she would want, and it was then she decided it was time to change the mood of the questioning. He was asking something she realized she wanted very much to be involved in, but all of a sudden her mouth went dry, and she turned away from him to hide confused feelings.

"I don't know, Mitch, I've never done this kind of decorating. And it would be up to the woman who was going to live here as to how it should be done, I would think. Every woman has such different tastes in such personal areas of a home." She felt a tugging at her heart that she didn't understand, a yearning that made her quickly walk away into the living room to sit in front of the fire.

He followed her and sat on the floor beside her, his long legs stretched out toward the merrily leaping flames. "Well, I'm in no hurry to finish those rooms. I have the one bedroom done, and one bath is pretty workable, so can manage for awhile, I guess," he replied.

He continued, "If you're not doing anything tomorrow night, would you like to take a drive around to see the Christmas lights? I understand from sis there are some fabulous home decorations, and she says each year gets better. Would you?"

He sounded so wistful and sincere about wanting to share this delight with her, she could not refuse him. She also loved the lights, and when she accepted his invitation, felt the pulses within her suddenly starting to hammer a song in her heart. It wasn't that he was pushy or demanding of her time, just the opposite, he was very considerate of her, very thoughtful and gracious.

But now and again, she could see in his eyes what he was thinking and feeling, and knew that her soul was shining for him to see. She couldn't hide it.

She tried to fight it and ignore, it, but, she realized, it had been very difficult to refuse him on any invitation he had issued lately.

Their friendship evolved over the months in the mutual working relationship at the clinic. There were many shared interests and at the top of this list was nature and animals; beautiful crystal and art followed closely.

Their familiarity grew into an abiding love as they discovered little by little a need and respect for each other that drew them close. There was no forgetting the love that each had lost; each resolving in his and her own way the heartache of their memories.

They discussed it endlessly and discovered each knew they did not want to spend the rest of their life alone; and each knew there was no turning back of time in their life.

Mitch and Cathy were married the following Fall in her small hometown family church.

It seems she was unable to refuse him that invitation as well.

CHAPTER TWELVE

"Mitch, I'm so nauseated this morning. I must be getting that flu that's going around. I'm going to stay home today," Cathy stated one morning. "It's a beautiful Spring day, and maybe I've got, ha-ha, Spring fever."

"All right, Cathy. It's very windy and cool today and it's probably better if you don't go outside if you have a fever. Stay warm. Promise?" He felt her forehead.

"Yes, worrywart, I promise," she replied, giving his cheek a loving pat.

After Mitch had left for the clinic, Cathy took a shower, and changed into a light sweater and slacks. Humming to herself, she tied a silk scarf around her hair and went to the garage for the car, then drove into the city to another clinic across town.

"Well, Jim, am I right? Tellme, tellme, before I barf all over your carpet," Cathy badgered.

"It wouldn't be the first time, Cathy, if you did barf all over the carpet. That's why this is a cleanable carpet," Dr Jim Thompson, OB-GYN, laughingly observed. "And yes, congratulations, you're right. You are a little over two months pregnant. Mitch doesn't know yet, does he? When are you going to give him the good news?"

Cathy was jumping up and down with excitement, "Tonight, Jim. I'll tell him tonight." She reached out and gave jaunty Dr Thompson a hug and took out of the office like it was on fire, hearing his roar of delight follow her.

"Helen," he called out his door, "call Cathy tomorrow and set up an appointment for one month from now. She was just too excited today to remember to do it," he told the nurse. With a big grin on his jovial face, he turned to the next examining roomand his next possible mother-to-be.

When Mitch came home that evening, he stated, "You must be feeling a lot better, Cathy. When I saw you this morning you even looked a little green. Taking the day off did you a world of good. You really look... very sweet tonight, all shiny and bright."

He set a brown briefcase onto the foyer table and turned to her. "I tried to call you this morning, and no answer. Were you sleeping and have the phone turned off or something?" His voice sounded tired and yet concern for her was uppermost in his words.

"Mitch, come here to me, please," she urged with a kittenish soft look, and outstretched arms. He walked over to her, and she reached up, pulled his face to her and kissed him.

"Hey, kiddo," he objected as he pulled back slightly from her, "I know we share and share alike, but I don't really want your flu."

"Silly, I don't have the flu. I have something better that's going to last a lonnnnnnng time, and I'm going to look green in the mornings for awhile, and…" She stopped, looking at him with a smile on her face as wide as a banana is long, then started to sing the soft and melodious, "Rock-a-bye-baby in the tree-top…."

It had taken only a moment of what Cathy was singing to sink in and as she started the second line of the ditty, she found herself suddenly engulfed in his arms. He swung her gleefully around the room, shouting and dancing with unabashed joy. "Yeh? Yeh? You're…? We're…? Oh, Cathy, my darling wife, I'm so deliriously happy," he cried to her when she nodded her affirmation. And he was very quickly, literally, crying tears of joy. Cathy had never before felt this connected to, or loved by, anyone else in her life.

The next few months were joyous and also so very interminable. Cathy felt her body to be a lopsided balloon, and her back ached almost constantly when she was up and around. She was testy and irritable, and Mitch couldn't do enough for her.

He did insist she quit working when she was six months, which was fine with her. She wanted to rework the spare bedroom into a nursery, and to do the designing of it herself, if possible. The images of whimsical panda bears, bunny's, kittens, puppies, and birds spoke volumes about the love of animals Cathy had, and she knew Mitch felt the same way. They were all humorously portrayed on the upper walls frolicking about a soft pale green meadow with multi-colored pastel flowers, while on the ceiling was a pale blue sky where a few cottony clouds billowed.

The purchasing of the baby furniture; acquiring the baby layette; showers that her co-workers and cousins arranged; and scores of little details that needed to be done occupied her days and Cathy moved through this time in a state of, Is this really happening to me? jubilation.

The picking out of names was the most fun, and the focus of the most heated discussions they had had on any subject.

From Mitch, "No Evan Junior for my son, nosireee," he shook his head, "maybe Michael Patrick, I like that—or, Steven Aloyss—after my father. Or," his eyes lit up, "after my grandpa George. He was always so great to me," he finished warmly.

"And, Cathy, how about Francis Howard, after your father? And, no contest, for a girl, Clara Julia, after our mothers. In my heart, anyway," he murmured.

"Okay, okay, you win for now," she conceded smilingly.

On the night their beautiful baby boy was brought into the world, the wind was howling and whipping rain into driven sheets, lightning lit up the darkness and thunder pounded outside the hospital room. But none of it impressed Cathy as she neither heard nor noticed it, but Mitch would glance once in a while out the window.

Mitch stayed with her throughout the entire delivery, and when the baby was finally presented to them all sweet and cuddled in a tiny blanket, Cathy dreamily introduced her son to Mitch, saying, "Meet Steven Francis, darling, and Steven, meet your father."

"Yes," Mitch breathed softly to her. "I like that name. It fits him somehow. Hello, sweet Steven Francis Mitchell. You sure are coming into the world on a stormy night. But then, ya' know?... the earth is always fresher after a rainstorm. And, you've made my whole world fresher already, dear little ones, both of you."

He wallowed in adoration of this baby, his son, and thanked his wife again and again for giving him such a gift.

Reluctantly, he kissed both of them goodnight. "Sleep now, Cathy, I'll see you in the morning."

Softly tiptoeing out of the room, Mitch danced down the hallway quietly stabbing his arms into the air in triumph, his softly hissed, "Yessssss!" skipping off the wall as he made his way to the car.

Cathy returned to work only part-time, for two years later their second son, Michael Evan, was born to as much fanfare and anticipation as little Stevie had been. This difficult birth was fated to be the last one for them, however, as there were many complications, and Cathy was rendered incapable of conceiving any more.

They savored every precious moment, and at the same time groused at the disturbance of their sleep; the interminable changes that each baby needed; the 'terrible two's' of Steven, and the disruption of just about any and all adult activities: Each had to admit they wouldn't change places with anyone in the world.

The next several years saw many changes at the clinic. They expanded into four examining rooms; added another radiologist—Dr Kevin Paulson; a secretary, and two more technologists were also added to the staff. Computers were at the brink of being the most accurate, the fastest and highly expensive technology to be issued into the medical field, and with this technology came deeper and more probing advanced studies into the human body.

There were seminars for Mitch and the other radiologists to attend; research and technical papers to read and write; and local Board meetings to attend of which Mitch was elected President for one year duration. Hours were spent reading and studying new advances that rapidly accumulated in the technical references that were issued monthly.

The tech's also had to keep up with the changing technology of their chosen field. Each had to attend lectures and seminars, and accrue points for proof of continuing education to retain their yearly license. These arduous requirements were mandatory, and all cared about being the best: Mitch, Cathy, and all the other personnel as well. They all took pride in their well-run organization, and realized they were among an elite group whose business had doubled again and again, the reward of efforts to show the patients and physicians they were committed to their welfare.

The Fire Chief called Dr John Sazama a little after midnight about the fire at the clinic, and John, in turn, called Mitch at 12:35 a.m. telling him about it and to get there quickly; John also called Dr Paulson.

When Mitch arrived, the Fire Chief said the smoke and water had invaded the whole of the building, but the worst of the fire was over and it had been contained to two examining rooms and two offices. It was still smoldering with small red and orange flickers licking out from under the fallen rubble, and firemen were still dousing them as they appeared. The back walls and roof were crumbled into tangled heaps of debris, and white clouds of smoke curled up from the depths of this refuse into the night air. The acrid smell of charred, blackened wood and other materials permeated the area.

As the still lingering small flames, and the lights from the fire and emergency trucks danced with the shadows in the driveway, Dr Sazama paced back and forth such as a tiger in a cage. He could not be reconciled with the fact that this had happened. All he could do was stare, totally stunned and shocked, into the disaster.

The fire investigators determined right away it was arson from accelerant markings found inside the side entrance from the parking lot. Heavy dark spots here and there in this lobby entrance showed a hotter fire had burned where kerosene or gas had been splashed and poured.

Mitch was beside himself. "Arson? Arson! Who the hell would do such a thing... and for God's sake, why?"

Who could do such a thing as to take away a thriving medical business and turn it into ashes? They had no enemies that were known to them; they had good working relationships with the referring physicians with only a few personality and minor clinical clashes. Patients had come and gone with only a few, also minor, glitches and disruptions.

"Nothing that should have led to something as drastic as this!" he gasped.

It was two days before they could adequately get into the building to estimate the amount of damage, and to see in better detail the direction and how badly the fire had progressed. Dr Sazama was crushed with the burden of what had happened. This clinic was his pride and joy, his dream and his life. Along with Mitch, and Dr Paulson, he went over the lists of materials and equipment no longer usable, and marked them off as lost for the insurance company.

Decisions would have to be made to safeguard the files and reports that could be salvaged; where to put them after investigators were finished was a problem that had to be taken care of as soon as possible.

Dr Sazama inquired, "Mitch, could we put these lists on your home computer and then run off copies for the insurance company?"

"Sure, John. I'll have Cathy type them in and do that. She said she could leave the kids with Shirley down the road so she can work uninterrupted and help with it."

They were lucky enough to find rooms in an office building a mile or so away from the clinic, and rented it for their work. It was convenient, protected, and roomy enough to store the boxes of x-ray files that the staff and tech's took over. Since everything had been still in the transition phase of being converted to computer from paper file, they still had drawer after drawer of card files. As these Card File records of patients in the front office had been spared, from these they would be able to determine which of the patient files were missing.

"Well, people," Dr Sazama said a few days later when he had called his staff together, "Looks like you're all on reduced pay for awhile until we can get things put back together again. Insurance is covering a lot of that, but not full pay. Sorry. Thanks for all your help in getting the files and records in some semblance of order so we can determine what's missing and there's not a lot of files gone since the storeroom was spared." He ran his hand wearily through his hair. "They've proven it was arson, but not who, so we'll just have to hope the police can come up with a person, or persons, and go on about getting this clinic up and running again, andsoforth. Any of you who needs to have full pay for living expenses, talk to me before you go looking for another job... we'll see what we can work out. I don't want to lose any of you, if possible, and we'll need your help again when we set things back up." He hunched his shoulders to try and relieve the knots, then waved his hand in dismissal toward the concerned employees as they muttered among themselves.

He was very tired from the long wearying hours and strain of the past week. Another two weeks and architectural blueprints were brought in by the firm who had done the renovation before, and a plan was started for the reconstruction.

Anger was fermenting in John, and he lashed out in frustration when he was told that it would be months before insurance would pay expenses for the restoration that needed to be done. "What the hell do we pay premiums for if we have to wait that long, would you please tell me?" His tirade was aimed at the insurance investigator sent by the company to verify the claims. "The police have proof that it's arson, where it started, about what time, and how. What more do you need, for crying-out-loud!"

"Yes, doctor, I understand, but they don't know who. How well do you know the people who work with you?" was the slick reply of the man.

"Who!" John exploded. "What...do you think perhaps one of us did it to claim the insurance?" He stood up and jabbed his finger at the man, "Maybe close the clinic down and just leave with the money, is that what you have in mind? Well, think again, buster, none of us would, or could, do anything like that. This franchise is set up so that cannot happen."

John was furious, not just at the man standing in front of him, but at the implication that any of his people was capable of such a hideous thing. It was taken personally by John Sazama, and it was with a great effort of will that he took control of his anger, and told the man in good old plain unvarnished English, but with the edge of a whiplash in his voice, "You had better get your act together, and get the money we need for our rebuilding in the mail ASAP, or you will be out one medical clinic as a client!"

But they didn't get the money. The monies needed would have to come from the partners own pockets, and from a bank loan. The insurance wouldn't settle yet.

All were a little worried because the perpetrator had not yet been found, or the reason for it happening at all. And as the days went by, the police were no further into solving the mystery than when they started. No one was seen loitering around the building, or suspicious cars or movement, and the investigators were dissatisfied in their efforts.

They interviewed everyone they could think of; neighbors across the street, up the street, down the street. Patients, and their personal physicians; the salesmen who had appointments in the previous days and that day were included. And again and again, they talked to the doctors about any strange person they could have had trouble with. They exhausted many possibilities, and came up empty. And they wanted an answer. Most of them, and their families, had had exams done at this clinic.

The days were long and tedious for the three doctors. They were taking advantage of the rebuilding time to go out of town and sometimes out of state to seminars and study/lectures on the new computer technology in equipment and services; they had decided to get the latest and most advanced machinery they could get to replace what was lost.

In between the trips, they oversaw the construction and reviewed the plans that included adding yet another specialty room. The tech's also were going to conventions, and volunteering their own time a couple hours each day as they monitored at the hospital department to learn how to operate the equipment, since the hospital had been able to install some of the latest machines very recently.

On a cold wintry night, several months later, not really paying close attention to the rambling and intermittent shouting of a rowdy fifteen-year-old high school boy who had been arrested on drug charges, the arresting officers' attention was popped into focus when the boy started mumbling about, "the hot ones I did, I show'd 'em all."

"What are you talking about, son?" the officer asked.

"Nothin', nothin'. You'll be sor'y you pulled me in, tha's all." His speech was slurred in the aftermath of the drugs, his eyes wide, glaring, and defiant, his body swaying and rocking in the chair the officer had put him in.

"Oh, I know. You're talking about the hot stuff you just mainlined, huh?" the officer queried of him.

At this the boy started laughing, a sound much like the mechanical laugh tracks that can be heard in a carnival; grating, high-pitched, and screeching.

"No, man, no!" the boy protested loudly. "I would never mainline...junk or nothin'." The boy continued to babble under his breath, "Man, but they were beautiful."

"Then you must have stolen the stuff you snorted, or popped, or whatever you did. Hey, you can get in big time trouble with... Who did you say you stole that stuff from?" the officer tested him.

"I din't steal nothin'!" the boy stormed defiantly.

At this the officer left the room to talk to his captain telling him what the boy had said about, 'the hot one's he did', 'he'll show'em all', and, 'they were beautiful'.

"I don't know, captain. I have a funny feeling about this kid. Tony is new to junk, especially the kind we found on him tonight. I just wonder if he's tied into the clinic fire somehow, and the other two warehouse fires that have occurred in the past couple months. He's not making any sense, but he may have slipped up just enough. What should I do with him?"

"Are his parents on the way, or someone responsible?" Captain McCallahan asked.

"No, they're 'out of town', the boy says, and we can't get ahold of them. Only the butler and his wife where the boy lives."

"Charge him with disorderly conduct, use of illegal drugs, possession of drugs and take him to Juvenile Mental Health at Zeller Center, and I'll get a court order to have him held in for observation. He's going to come down hard from that high he's on now, and he's going to need help. We'll hold him until we can find his parents, at least."

It was three days later when Mr and Mrs C. J. Robbins were ushered into the Captains office.The father sniffed disdainfully. "Where is our boy, Captain, and what have you done to him?"

The parents were dressed in expensive silk designer clothes with obviously very lavish and famous-label designed diamond jewelry: A brooch, attached to the bodice of her dress and a gold tie-tack fastened onto his tie, were both sparkling with diamonds.

His hair was slicked and shining; her hair streamlined into a smooth double-chignon at the nape of her neck; their tanned, streamlined bodies were erect and condescending.

Their haughty manner irritated the Captain. "It's taken you awhile to wonder or worry about where you son is, your only child, I've been told," the Captain admonished.

"We've been in the Bahamas, on... business," the father snorted, tweaking his nose at the odors of coffee and Danish rolls on a small table just outside the captains office door. "Besides, Tony is old enough to take care of himself."

"Is that so? Do you realize he's also old enough for possibly prison," he emphasized, "and under suspicion of arson? Not to mention the drugs that were found in his possession, and that he was high on."

At the mention of the word 'prison', the parents faces blanched, they looked at one another, and their demeanor changed immediately.

Captain John McCallahan did not initially like the artificial manner of the parents, but he pulled his professionalism around him, and told them where their boy was, and why. "I really think you'd better call a lawyer, your boy is in deep, deep trouble." He tried hard to hide his dislike for them.

During the first couple days at Zeller, Tony had come down hard from his trip on the drugs. When the fog began to clear—it was on the third day—the colors and images his mottled brain had been imagining were subdued and put into focus, he came to the realization of where he was and why.

"Mom, Dad, when did you get home... recently?" Tony asked of his parents.

The nurse had called them to his room when Tony wondered out loud to her about them.

"We've been here since this morning, dear. Didn't you know?" His mother stayed across the room, apart from him, brushing her green silk dress with her pale pink painted fingertips, then caressed the smoothness of her hair with the palm of her hand. She didn't move to hug or kiss her son. His angry father, scowling at him, stood beside her.

Unexpectedly, his father stomped across the room and stepped up close to where Tony sat, and in a grating voice asked him, "Have you done what they say you have, boy?"

"And what is that, Father?"

"That you... burned buildings. Is that true?"

"Yeah, I guess so," Tony replied in an offhand manner. "Had to do something to keep myself occupied at night. Big crowds are always around at a big fire, and I kinda liked that. Besides," he shrugged his shoulders, "fires are pretty awesome to watch. Have you ever been to one and watched it, Father? I mean, the colors are something else! And you get a little pot, or stuff, into you and watch a fire...? Man, is that one incredible trip!"

His mother objected in a whiny voice, "But you weren't alone, dear. Jamie has been with you all of the time since you were born."

"Yeah, I know, Mom, but a butler has a life of his own, too, you know, and Jamie..., oh, just forget it," he threw at them disgustedly.

All this was avidly listened to by his father hovering near him, and now he reached out and began to shake Tony by his shoulders; rage was beginning to redden his face. He shouted, "We give you everything you need. Why should you have to do such an atrocity as to burn a medical clinic, for heaven's sake!

And the others, the two warehouses? Did you do those? Were there any others, Tony? Answer me!"

His father's fury was frightening to Tony. "Just a couple of empty houses, I swear. No one was ever hurt in any of them."

Tony's face was turning white with foreboding. He had never seen his father in any strong emotion, especially this kind of wrath. The tears oozed from his wide eyes in fright, not remorse, for what he had done. He distorted his lithe young body in an attempt to release himself from his father's strong hands. When he beseeched his mother with his eyes, she looked away. His father saw the begging look, loosened his hold, than pushed him back into the chair. "What are we going to do with you, Tony?" he groaned dejectedly.

Tony's parents saw to it that he had plenty of money, and never wanted for anything, except the one thing he wanted the most, their love and time. But they were too busy with their own affairs, and had no time for his emotional needs. He was fifteen, and this urge to connect with his parents had been chasing him all these years since he was old enough to realize his life was different than the other kids in school.

Being a policeman could have its rewards when a case comes together and an answer found.

Tony, hanging his head, but with his parents, informed the police telling them what he had done. He droned, "I brought gasoline in a pint jar and stashed it in thick bushes close to the side door of the clinic. Then I slipped inside the building and hid before they locked up for the night, then propped the door open, brought in the jar of fuel, splashed it around, lit it, and ran like hell; it took only a couple of minutes and it was done. The empty warehouses and other houses were easy to get into."

Tony glanced at his mother, and was startled to see tears running down her cheeks.

It was elected to leave him in Zeller for therapy and drug rehabilitation in exchange for reduced charges since he was only a kid of fifteen, this was his first arrest, and there had only been loss of property and no deaths or injuries. The juvenile court agreed. There were not too many options open.

It took a long while for the therapists to get Tony to realize that his mother and fathers' lack of loving care was not his fault. During these sessions, he finally found out that—in his adolescent need—he had done the fires for attention, his parent's attention. "I figured if I did something drastic enough, they'd have to notice I was alive, wouldn't they?" And, "Then I did the drugs to hide the guilt I felt for doing the fires." It was a no-win cycle he had been caught up in. And he had gotten their notice; he had made them listen, even if it was for a few, very brief visits.

His parents then left for the Bahamas again, leaving Tony to face his darkest hours alone. They had agreed to compensate the owners of the property's for their losses over what insurance would pay, and felt their duty done.

He grew up and turned sixteen there, really came closer to manhood in those few short weeks with the personnel helping. His every material need was taken care of. His parents were back a couple of times to visit with him briefly, dump more money into his care, then left again assuring themselves Tony did not need them right there with him.

By then, he wanted to grow up. He wanted to not have to need them anymore, to want their presence and assurances; they didn't give that anyway, so what was he missing? He would always feel a capricious ache inside that he now knew would never be filled.

It took a total of seven weeks of therapy before Tony could face anyone. His image of self-worth was shattered for a long time when he began to fully comprehend what he had done in setting the fires, the drugs also having torn him into bits and pieces. But he struggled, many dedicated professionals helping him, and the burning desire to come up from the hole he had fallen into became his lifeline. Little by little his reflection in the mirror grew visible to him again, and he could look at himself without flinching.

There was no longer any feeling for his parents; he neither hated them nor loved them, he felt…nothing. He could be polite to them, he had always been courteous. Tony did not look forward to their visits anymore, only was surprised when all of a sudden they appeared without notice.

They still insisted on pushing money into his care, and had increased the huge trust fund set up for him to draw on when he was eighteen. In their minds he would then be an adult, and except for the monies they would always share with their only child, their obligations and responsibility for him were ended.

He knew, if, and when, he would ever need more for legitimate causes, they would help him, but, he also knew, he would never ask.

In all the turmoil he was going through, his physical care, his emotional well-being, and moral and spiritual lessons were still left to strangers. His parents had felt obligated enough to send a very large check to the clinic, to pay some of the costs for the building and equipment that insurance did not cover. Tony could be grateful to them for that.

CHAPTER THIRTEEN

Cathy and Mitch were shocked at the revelation about Tony. He had worked at their ranch helping to take care of the livestock, feeding them, exercising the horses. He played with the children as though they were his brothers, and at times led them in 'daredevil' rides on Ranger and Bitsy, and sometimes, getting all of them into mischievous trouble.

Mitch approached Cathy one morning. "Hon, what do you think about bringing Tony out to the ranch to live. We could use the extra hand since you're back to work fulltime again, and he could use the home. What do you think? I don't know if he'll even want to, but we could talk to him about it. He could finish high school, at least, and get his diploma, and then do whatever he wants after that."

"I don't know, Mitch, we have our children to think of. He's always been good with them, but...." Cathy left the implication hanging in the air.

"Yeah, I know. I've been talking to the physicians at Zeller, and they feel he's ready for some outside responsibility. He needs to know he can be trusted again. He's still not feeling too good about himself."

"But do we trust our children to him to test his responsibility? I don't know," she retorted doubtfully. "And you, do you truly believe your anger about the fire at the clinic is over enough to handle his being here?"

"Well, I've found out a lot about him and the life he's had to live, and I really feel sorry for the kid. He hasn't had a home life at all except for the butler and his wife taking care of him and the house and such. His parents have been gone all his life since about his first grade in school. When he started school, they started traveling and haven't come home since or taken him with them except for a few summer vacations."

He took in a deep breath. "I have never—never—seen such selfish behavior of parents in my life as what those two have done to Tony. Any training for life, any love, has had to come from the butler, Jamie and his wife Nora, and I have to give them credit, they've done a good job. Tony had never been in trouble before. But he's growing up and needs more than what they can give him now."

In the end, they compromised. Tony would come to the ranch for awhile and would be supervised at all times, especially with the children, going back to school through the week. They would trial-run it and see if this was what he wanted also.

But Tony had no doubts. He was exultant to be starting his life again, and the two boys greeted him with loud gladness jumping all over him.

"Tony, Tony, take us for a ride, please. Momma, can Tony take us for a ride, please, puhleeze?" the boys clamored.

"All right, fella's, calm down, calm down for goodness sake and give Tony a chance to catch his breath," she laughed. "What about it, Tony, do you want to saddle up the horses and take these rambunctious cowboys for a ride? If you want to ride Ranger with Michael, Steven has been doing pretty good on Bitsy riding by himself, but keep him close."

"Yes, m'am, I'd like that a lot. And we'll go slow and easy, too, I promise!" He was flush with happiness, grinning as big as possible, not daring to believe this was really happening to him.

"Stay close in the front pasture, Tony, the weather looks like it could change suddenly, and I don't want the boys to get drenched if it does," she called to him as the three bounced out the door, laughing and yelling to each other. She watched them anxiously, really wanting it to work for Tony.

Tony was excited, and proud, that she was trusting him with the boys and the horses even if it was a slow walk in the front pasture. After all he had done, he wasn't sure she would ever truly trust him again. When he had talked about it in his therapy sessions, he had realized she was the closest to an emotional nurturing woman he knew. There was nothing he wouldn't do to please the woman calling out the door to him, and was very willing to work hard to earn her trust. Jamie's wife had done her job in her sober and benevolent manner, but he had felt no warmth or affection from her from his toddler years on up.

And, as Cathy had anticipated, the storm broke while the boys were on the farthest side of the pasture, close to the creek, and they had to hurry to get into the barn before they were completely drenched.

Laughing and whooping with glee, the boys on their steeds canter into the warmth and dryness of the shelter. Dismounting, then unsaddling the mounts took just a short time.

"Come on, Tony, let's go to the house," the boy's shouted in unison.

"Hey, short-stuffs, we have to wait until the rain stops a bit or we'll get soaked. We have to rub down the horses anyway. We can't leave them wet, so just pick up a brush and we'll get done sooner. I'll call your mom on the intercom and tell her we're okay here in the barn."

Cathy was relieved to hear from him, "Tony, just stay there while the rain is so heavy. Come on back up to the house when it lets up."

"Okay, Mz Mitchell, we have to rub down the horses anyway."

It was a terrible storm, the lightning and thunder fierce.

It rattled and shook the buildings with each booming salvo, and seemed to pass directly over the ranch, the clouds glowering and confronting anything that challenged its temper and authority.

And its teammate, the wind, finished it by daring anything to stop it from squealing through and around the cracks, holes and corners it found in the barn and house.

Oh, dear, this is flashflood kind of rain, I think, Cathy worried. I hope the bridge on the lane holds. There's going to be a lot of water come down out of those hills. No, now I'm worrying about nothing! There's been this kind of rain before and it's weathered it all right. I'm just being paranoid, but I just wish Mitch were here on this side of the creek. What time is it? He should be coming any time now, I hope. Come on, stop it! The boys are safe where they are, and Mitch will be, too. He knows this road and bridge better than anyone.

And her prediction was true. Mitch came through the rain about an hour later. It was still pouring, and she was sure the boys were starting to get restless and antsy being cooped up in the barn so long. When he pulled into the attached garage, Cathy met him.

"Mitch, will you drive down to the barn and bring the boys up to the house? Tony is surely done rubbing down the horses by now, and I'm sure they're as anxious to get back up here as I am. Thanks, dear."

"Sure, and if Tony hasn't already fed the stock, I can do that while I'm there. Shouldn't take too long. Some rain, huh?"

The creek was already rising rapidly, the water pouring out of the hills to the north.

Mitch, Tony, and the boys rounded up the llamas, goats, and cows and herded them over the bridge and into the upper pasture near the barn.

Boots, nipping and yapping at the animals tried to hurry them up, and only caused them to scatter more.

Mitch frustratingly yelled over the pounding rain, "Steven, Michael, one of you catch Boots, and stop him from 'helping'. How the hell did he get out here to begin with."

Turning to Tony he roared, "It's much higher ground here, and they'll be safer if the creek goes out of its banks like it looks like it could." Mitch hollered, "We better get them into the pens and barn now while we can. I don't think this is going to stop for awhile."

And the rain did not stop for hours, coming in sheets, then slacking a little, then driving hard against the windows again.

It was a huge storm front and all forecasts told them it would be with them for a long while.

When the boys and the two men were dried off, Cathy had a meal ready for them.

"Come on, sit down and eat, you all must be starving by now… oh, dear."

It was at that precise moment the lights went out. This had happened in the past but Cathy was not prepared for it. She muttered all the way to the pantry in the dark where she fumbled in drawers and a cabinet to locate and bring out the candles and oil lamp.

After lighting all of them and placing them in strategic places, Mitch acknowledged, "Well, this is kind-of nice, eating by soft candlelight. Right, boys?"

"Yeah, right, Dad, now we can't watch T.V., and what else is there to dooo," whined the two young boys.

Tony interjected, "Hey, come on, guys, we'll find something fun to do."

"Yeah, like… what?"

"Well, after the dishes are done, I'll teach you to play cards, or maybe Parcheesi with dice. I brought my game board along with the dice and pieces. Want to try? It's fun, and you don't need electricity to play them."

It was very difficult to drag the two young boys away from their game with the dice and playing pieces when it was time for bed.

"Come on, hit the sack you two. Tony has other things to do, I'm sure," Cathy admonished with a smile.

Later, when the boys were fast asleep, Cathy approached Tony.

"Thanks, Tony, for saving us from the terrors of two little ones who have 'nothing to dooo'," mimicked Cathy. "And for helping Mitch round up the stock. I just have a feeling we're not going to be able to get across that bridge safely by morning." She stepped close to him and put her hand on his arm.

To her utter amazement, Tony began to cry. Not the sobbing of a child, but the shaky tears of a boy who was still reeling emotionally from the past few months, and who thought then his whole life was going down the drain. He suddenly realized these people cared about him and showed it. Even after all that had transpired in what he had done, he knew without a doubt they cared about him.

He acknowledged her words with a self-conscious nod of his head, then turned his head away to hide the moistness that had come against his will to his eyes, but not soon enough; Cathy caught the glint of the moisture in the candlelight, and guessed that he was embarrassed. She turned and walked back to her chair.

"I think I'll go to bed now, too. Goodnight, Mz Mitchell, Doc Mitch. I'll get up early to go check on the livestock."

"Goodnight, Tony. Sleep well," Cathy and Mitch responded to him.

The storm raged on through the night, blowing fiercely at times, at times the rain gentle and pattering on the roof. Tony slept fitfully, tossing and turning on his cot in the spare-room.

He awakened with a start when a thunderbolt was thrown down with a savage crash, the booming of it making the house shudder with its impact. Flashes of lightning were alarming in their intensity and brightness, the thunder following in a cacophony of drum-rolls that was, at times, almost constant. This was a storm blitz following a storm furor, all madly transpiring in the middle of the night, raging on and on seemingly without letup for hours.

The morning dawn was soggy and gray; the rain had finally stopped; the wind had stopped. Only a gentle breeze moved the saturated, sodden trees in the front yard. The sun could not yet break through the still overcast sky, but the birds had awakened with a song, celebrating the finish of an all night siege that shook them as they slept, and now they were ready to refresh themselves with an early worm or two which the storm had flushed from their deep burrows.

Tony was up with them, dressed and out the door before anyone else in the house was awake. The mess the storm created with downed limbs and debris scattered all over was barely noticed by him; he was concerned about the animals. He found the llama's huddled up against the side of the barn under a large overhang... they're all right. The goats were in a pen close beside them and had been sheltered in a small three-sided lean-to.

The two cows and two horses had been put into the barn, and all had come through just fine, along with the six kittens and their momma cat. The two ducks spotted Tony and waddled down noisily honking their greeting, and to get their handout of corn. They probably found a small place for shelter under the large hay wagon stored behind the barn, Tony thought as he reached into a bag for their breakfast of the corn. Everywhere he walked the mud and gunk tried to suck the boots from his feet.

When he came around the corner of the barn and gazed down the hill to the creek, he stared in open-mouth shock. There was no creek anymore. There was a raging river many times as wide as the mild wandering creek had been, and when his eyes followed the course of the madly rushing water to where the bridge stood, he saw the bridge gallantly holding onto unseen footholds as the water swirled around and over the floor of it, with only the top one-half of the sturdy wooden tree-post hand-railing visible. He turned and fled back to the house slipping and sliding in the muck in his haste.

"Mz Mitchell, Doc Mitch, come quick! Come look!" he screamed as he ran. "You have to come see the creek. It's... it's... hurry, come see the creek!"

The swollen water wasn't going to go away any time soon, but his yell carried an urgency to it as if it might. He was awe-struck, shocked, and somewhat... no, very, terrified at what he saw.

When he had finally aroused the sleepy family and they were assembled outside, Tony's urging carried them to the edge of the yard to peer down at the creek. They were astounded, and shocked wide-awake at what they saw, such as Tony had been.

"Steven, Michael, you are not to go out of this yard, do you understand? That water is dangerous, and there could be holes it has dug out, and the current could be fierce. Do you two understand that you are not to go anywhere near that water?"

Cathy looked at her two offspring, and tried to decide if her words had stuck into their heads. Recognizing the exploratory mindset they both had, and knowing they barely understood the meaning of the word 'fear', she tried to inject into them this water was not to be explored; Mitch and Tony also echoed her. Promises were extracted from both to only watch from afar, and to give everyone running accounts of what was happening—from the yard..

Suddenly grasping the situation from his perspective, Steven cried joyously, "Good, Mom, no school. How 'bout that?" as he jumped up and down in glee . "Can't get across to go to school. Yayyyy! I'm going to ride Ranger around. He's probably pretty nervous from the storm last night. Tony, will you help me saddle up? Mom, Dad, is it okay?"

Cathy couldn't resist the open-eyed, exuberant enthusiasm of her oldest, and knew she couldn't keep the boys cooped up in the house, or even the yard, until the creek went down, no matter how much she wanted to.

She glanced quickly at Mitch, "All right. But Tony, keep them close in the upper pasture. You know what I'm saying."

He shook his head enthusiastically, "Yes, M'am, I do know."

Ranger and Bitsy seemed ready for the exercise when the boys showed up in the barn. They weren't used to being shut up for this length of time and when Tony tried to put the saddles on, they danced and skittered sideways in the stall anxious to be going.

Finally, both horses were saddled and he led them out the doorway into the sun that was starting to break through the gray clouds.

True to his word, Tony walked ahead of both horses keeping tight hold of the reins, one in each hand, to prevent them from going to their habitual pasture which was on the other side across the bridge. He didn't want them to head that way or get close to the swirling, rushing water.

But Ranger was feisty this morning and Steven, in his young enthusiasm, kept inciting him further, digging and pounding his heels into Rangers' flank.

"Faster, Tony, let Ranger go faster. He's jumpy this morning and wants to run. Can I run him, Tony, please?"

Without warning, a weakened tree limb snapped and came crashing down alongside the horse, and Ranger reared his head, prancing in fright. The rein snapped loose from Tony's hand, and Ranger, finding himself free, was off and running.

Tony screamed, "Stevie, grab the rein...! Grab the rein!"

He reached up and quickly plucked Mike unceremoniously from Bitsy, stood him on the ground, and swung himself onto the saddle in one smooth motion, digging his heels into the mare to charge after the runaway Ranger.

He could see Steven try to grab the reins, but having to hang onto the saddle horn with one hand and reach forward on a neck that was heaving up and down made that impossible to do with his short arms.

"Oh, Lord, make him stop," Tony prayed. "Please, Lord, help me stop that horse before it's too late." He prayed without knowing what words he was saying, or that he was saying them.

In between, he yelled, "Stevie, hold on, boy, hold on tight! I'm coming!"

His teeth clamped tightly together, he entreated Bitsy, "You're as fast as Ranger. Get him, girl, get him."

Bitsy seemed to sense the urgency Tony was putting into her, and flew across the meadow as she had never run before, mud flying behind her hooves. Tony could see Ranger had now swung slightly to the right heading for the bridge and coming ever closer to the waters' edge. He guided Bitsy directly toward the bridge in instinctive anticipation, pushing desperately to cut Ranger off.

They met within the waters' edge, very close to the embankment leading down and onto the bridge. Bitsy was edged advantageously in front of Ranger. Tony pulled up sharply on the reins digging his knees hard against her sides. Her front legs pawed the air wildly.

This near meeting of such forward power forced Ranger to also slash the air and swing around as both horses danced crazily. Wild, agitated hooves splayed water in every direction momentarily causing Tony to lose sight of Steven.

Steven, never having had a good hold, slid backwards as though the horses' backend was a slide, his legs conforming to the curve of Rangers rump. He landed on his back with a hard thud a couple of feet into the rippling mass of water, parting the water with a splash, legs wide apart and flailing the air.

As Bitsy spun around, Tony caught sight of Steven and watched in wide-eyed horror as Steven, in what seemed to be slow motion, tilted, his body turning over and almost disappearing under the water.

Bitsy was under control. Tony threw the rein forward and slid off her back in a fluid action.

"Stevie, Steven, grab my hand! Grab my hand!" Tony shrieked as he leaned forward over the wetness swirling in front of his feet. He could not enter it.

There was seemingly no undercurrent here where the waters bounded coarsely over and against the slightly sloping meadow.

But the wind had been knocked out of Steven. Unable to breathe, he pushed a hand against the bottom and raised his head sideways, struggling to get his face above the water. Twisting his body and forcing himself to sit upright in the moving flow, he quivered, gasping and heaving the choking fluid from his mouth and airway. He gasped a deep breath, coughing and choking.

Tony looked at the water closely. He guessed it to be less than a foot deep, which seemed insurmountable. He could see the grasses bent over with the waters movement. His heart pounded quite fearfully; his legs trembled; his body shuddered with terror. With great resolve and tenacity, he managed to control his unnerving panic and formed a new-found gritty determination. He focused totally on Steven. He had to get Steven out of there!

Putting one foot forward, he stepped into the water, stepped again with the other foot, than stepped again, and again.

When near enough, he extended his hands into the coldness, and grabbed Steven under his arms. With the effortless ease of strength built up by fear, he pulled Stevie up into his arms and carried him step by step back to the safety of the higher meadow, away from the dangerous waters.

Michael had raced into the house to tell Mitch and Cathy what was happening, and it was only a couple of moments until they were kneeling beside the boys. They had taken one horrified look and raced down the lane leading to the bridge, ordering Mike to stay put where he was in the yard as they ran.

They had seen it all as it happened, a nightmare come to life.

Both horses pawing the air...Steven sliding backwards off the rump of Ranger... Tony's leap from Bitsy.... It was the worst few moments of their lives.

Steven was still coughing and sputtering when they reached the two boys. Little by little he was getting his breath back.

"Mom, Dad, it's... all my fault," he gasped. "I kept pounding on Ranger... with my heels..., and Tony has told me and told me... I'm not... supposed to do that." He tried for a bigger breath.

"I kept digging... at him and tried to..., wanted... to, run him. Tony didn't let me, ...honest, Mom," he beseeched. "A tree limb...broke and...Ranger reared up and...he started running."

A deep cough escaped Steven. "He broke loose from Tony." Steven was breathless as he desperately told his tale. Tony mustn't be blamed for what had happened! Tony was a big brother to him and might be sent away, and he couldn't stand the thought of that happening!

Tony, still breathing heavily from his exertion and with tears of relief running down his face, sat on the ground only a couple short feet away. He could hear Steven telling his parents what had happened and he shuddered. Steven was safe.

He had stepped into his most dreaded fear, water, and had conquered it for Stevie's sake. He hung his head then as the tears flowed unabashedly and it was only a moment before Cathy and Mitch were hugging and holding him and making sure he was all right as well.

It took almost one week before the creek was down far enough to be safe to cross the bridge. Mitch and Cathy no longer had any reservations about Tony being a responsible person, and took him into their family to live as one of their own, and the two younger boys were jubilant.

Cathy told him, "As soon as I can get supplies, you're going to have to help me redo the spare-room into your own bedroom and we'll make it over to whatever you would like it to be."

Engineer friends of Mitch came to inspect the bridge, and found it to be structurally as sound as ever. The pilings were very deep, and were holding as well as before the flooding.

There was some washout where the water had dug out the topsoil and widened the creek a couple of feet on either end of the bridge, but this could be refilled and fixed with fill-dirt, wire mesh and large rocks laid on top to slow the water should this flood again. Re-grading the gravel roadway on both sides of the bridge and bringing it back to its normal track was a major priority, and they promised to have heavy equipment out to them as soon as they could, two or three weeks at the most.

Life soon returned to a normal tempo; the boys were back in school. Mitch and Cathy had returned to work at the clinic, and the livestock had finally been transferred over to the lower pasture again through the day.

The following years were of a normal family building, learning, loving, and sometimes squabbling. The boys were growing up and at times it was a difficult process.

CHAPTER FOURTEEN

When the pain in his upper abdomen stayed there and kept building, Mitch said he had, "just an ulcer Cathy...I'm taking medicine for it." But after two weeks, the pain didn't go away, and he finally had to submit to some testing.

One week later when they were concluded, he and Cathy sat, stunned, in the office of his close associate and friend, Doctor Bernie Malcolm.

"Are you sure, Bernie? Positive? I can't believe this."

His voice low and wavering on the brink of hysteria, his hand crept into Cathy's hand, and he clung to it for support, and to keep from falling to the floor in a kicking, screaming rage of denial.

"Well, from all the tests done so far, that's what it looks like, Mitch. I'm sorry."

Bernie turned and walked to the window and looked out, not seeing anything because his frowning eyes were clouded and wet. "Maybe you would want to go to Mayo's or somewhere else to confirm it. They would have the latest in testing procedures, Mitch. There really is no other tests or treatment available here that I can do."

Mitch had taken all the tests required, the many nuclear medicine scans, the ultrasound scans, the blood testing, and x-rays. They all came back with the same-sounding report:

"A tumor in the pancreas... consistent with a malignancy."

"Cancer of the pancreas."

"Pancreatic carcinoma."

"Cells consistent with a malignancy, most likely of the pancreas."

The big C A. The wordings were phrased differently, but they all meant the same thing. There couldn't be a mistake.

"But, God, let there be a mistake! Let this death sentence not be meant for me," he prayed desperately. "I want to see my boys grow up, to hold my wife in my arms. I want to feel the sunshine, smell the rain and make snow angels. Please, Lord, is there any way around this?" His tears and anger were wrenching to his soul.

He tried every way he knew to make a deal with his Lord, but the answer was always the same, the reports never changed.

"Cathy, we need to go over some things. Can you come into the office for a little while?" He motioned for her to shut the door.

Mitch was sitting in his home office with papers seemingly scattered haphazardly around him on the large desktop, yet each stack had their purpose and story. He methodically took each stack in its turn. He needed to show each piece to Cathy to make sure she understood its use.

When he was finished with the litany and she had nodded her head in understanding and attached written notes to some of them, she then walked to the cold and empty fireplace, laid her head against the dark wooden mantle and cried; sobbing, despairing, frustrated, and very anguished tears.

He walked up behind her, put his arms around her, leaned his head on the back of hers, kissing her hair and caressing her.

"I'm sorry, Cathy my darling, for everything," he whispered.

At this, she swung around in his arms and clung to him, weeping openly and heavily, the first time since the news had hit them in Bernie Malcolm's office ten days ago. There had been tears all along, but now both of them burst loose and their emotions could not be controlled.

"Oh, Mitch, what are we going to do?"

He had accepted his fate. He had already gone through the "why me?" stage, and it had churned up resentment against the God he had loved all his life, and resentment was not a thing his heart would tolerate. He prayed a lot of prayers for his cross to be taken away, and the answer he had gotten inside his being was, it is your cross and it is meant to be this way.

Technology, therapy's, and surgery's had not, as yet, advanced enough to give him any hope or assurance of being healed.

It was typical of Mitch to be concerned for her welfare more than his own and worked at getting everything that needed to be done, done. He rested easier after that, but Cathy could not be consoled or accepting.

He had explained to her that Tony was financially independent, thanks to his parents truly magnanimous trust fund when he had turned eighteen. Steven and Michael needed to be provided for, and his partnership in the clinic was set up so they would continue to receive payments spread out over the next ten years in a buyout process from the other partners. Cathy still planned to continue working for awhile to accrue enough time for retirement benefits. With all of it, they were going to be financially all right.

It was the rest of it that was going to be difficult...so very, very difficult. And the time passed too swiftly for her, not swift enough for him. He struggled hard to retain what he could, taking the hypo's only when he absolutely had to kill the wracking pain that brought tears of agony to his face; the sight and sound indelibly burned into Cathy's heart.

She was lying awake, somehow feeling and knowing without knowing how, his time was near. His breathing was different, his body more relaxed than for a long time now. She was holding him, looking at him, caressing the top of his hair barely touching him as every movement, until these moments, seemed to create spasms of hurting in his body. He had refused to spend his last days in a hospital, and Cathy could not disregard his request. His mind was still with him, flash-

114

ing brilliant at times.

On the early morning of his deliverance, he opened his eyes and looked up at Cathy with a smile, then died peacefully curled in Cathy's arms, the way he wanted to. She held him for awhile afterwards; her lover, her husband, her friend, knowing this was the last time for forever, the tears flowing down her face and onto his. So quiet, so still, so peaceful, so pain-free now.

This last month there had been a lot of suffering the drugs could not abate.

His wonderful face, so full of joy and happiness before the illness, was drawn and ashen, his eyes surrounded by dark shadows and hidden deep in the crevices of a sunken and hollowed face.

She finally slipped her arm out from under his neck, kissed him sorrowfully, and went to call the boys.

They were all awake for some reason even though it was 2:10 in the morning. Does the specter of death so near permeate the very air that is breathed, somehow telling everyone within its immediate boundaries that it is time, so, be awake and watchful?

All three knew without being told why Cathy had come to their room. Each in his turn, faced it with a hug for their mother, then when she was gone from the room, pulled the covers over their heads and wept into their pillows.

She had asked each one if he wanted to come to the bedroom to see him one last time at home before he would be taken away.

Each came when he had regained some composure, knelt beside his father and said his goodbye. And Tony considered him his father. He could not feel anything for, and barely knew, his real father. This man he knew he loved very much, and also knew he had been loved in return.

In only five months time, Mitch was gone. It had been seventeen years of a very happy marriage.

CHAPTER FIFTEEN

Without the wonderful laugh, humor and zest for living that Mitch had had to keep her going, Cathy's tempo of living had sagged into a limbo of routine. Go to work, go home, eat, try to sleep, up to work, home, eat, try to sleep—other than the nights she was at a game.

The boys' many activities in their schools helped her to cope. The basketball, football, baseball—Mitch had loved them all, and had instilled a respect for the games into Cathy and the boys. She had never been that much of a fan or interested before Mitch in any of them, but she went to all of them now. It wasn't the same to the boys, but it helped them to see her there in the stands.

Two years, then four years were swiftly gone. Steven had graduated high school, and was in his last year of college at a university in Illinois, working toward his dream of becoming a teacher and coach. Michael was in his second year at a different university in southern Illinois, and taking courses in preparation for and pursuing his aspiration of following his father in medicine. Tony had graduated college and entered pre-med studies for veterinary school, his avocation of being a veterinary doctor slowly becoming a reality.

Two years later when Michael finished his fourth year at the university, Cathy decided she needed to get away and try to figure what she was going to do now. The boys were all into their own lives, as it should be, and loneliness can be very—lonesome.

Besides, she was having these disturbing dreams lately….Why now? Why is Joe coming back into my thoughts? Into my Dreams? Into my waking thoughts, and sleeping dreams? She still pined for Mitch, but he was gone forever. He still lived in her heart through their sons whenever she looked at them, or talked to them, or heard a trace of Mitch's laugh in theirs.

Joe is, where? Is he still living, is he still...? Oh, Lord, he has to be married and have a family just as I have had by now. But would he? No, he couldn't father his own family, unless his wife had had children from someone else… or they could have adopted. He didn't marry me because of his job, but he could have married someone else later in life.

Surely, he's not still doing the same job. Surely he has retired from that by now, and gone to a more wise or sane endeavor, or had been promoted out of it.

More sane endeavor? He has never considered his military profession as anything but a tough job, and neither had she when she understood why he was doing it.

Certainly, there was an element of vengeance there, but it was something he had to do and it wasn't just for himself. I remember he must have been highly trained in this career, and I feel he must have done it very well.

The least of her feelings for his profession was of it being an insane, unacceptable one for him to do.

I have to get away. Go somewhere and just get away by myself for a short while. Think about my life; think about what I'm going to do; think about my retirement from the clinic and all the free time now. Volunteering, yes, volunteering is good and something that can fill in the hours.

Keep around people and noises, sounds of music and laughter, and even tears; sounds that can make me feel alive and useful and needed. Hospital children's wards always need help, always are looking for someone to be near the little ones when their parents can't be. Yes, I love children, and I could start there.

She remembers, It has been almost eight years since Mitch is gone. Good heavens, almost thirty years since parting from Joe.

It was hard to imagine, hard to think about, but she did think of her love for both of them. The differences between them, and the sameness, in that both had loved her very much.

This morning a stop at the AAA office for brochures, maps and information for trips was the first thing on her agenda.

She had no idea where it was she wanted to go, or do, but somewhere, just to get away. A bus sightseeing trip to Europe sounded so good to her.

She had always wanted to tour Europe; Rome, Venice, the Swiss Alps, the tulip fields of Holland, and castles of Germany, Bavaria, and Belgium.But a bus tour meant crammed into a small zone with a lot of strangers for a lot of hours, and that's not what she had in mind. A driving tour of the same area was considered, except she was a little too timid to drive in foreign countries by herself.

A cruise! Right here in the leaflet it explains about the cruise to Alaska. She didn't remember picking up this particular pamphlet. Oh, yes, the look and coloring of the ship and glaciers on the cover had attracted my eye, and she had put it as an afterthought into the bag with the others.

Why not a cruise? It has people all around, but I wouldn't be jammed in with them for hours; I wouldn't be committed to sitting and doing small talk with a seatmate who holds no interest to me. I could be my myself if I want; sit in the lounges by myself if I want; spend time reading on the deck if I want; or just stay in my stateroom if I need to cry. Yes, a cruise is definitely the way I'm going to go. But Alaska?

When talking to the travel agent the next day, she was assured Alaska was big for a tourist cruise in July. It was a beautiful time of year, most of the snow having melted from winter. "Denali National Park is also a must-see for you to venture into," the agent said.

He told her, "One of the cruise packages takes you along the Inside Passage, with stops at several of the cities; Ketchikan, Juneau, Skagway, Sitka, Whittier, and Fairbanks."

She booked many side tours at each stop. Her travel agent pointed out to her the many places and things to see and do, and she read in the brochures about the fish hatchery's, Mendenhal Glacier with its beautiful blue walls of ice after it has 'calved' an ice floe, totem poles in Ketchikan, stage shows in Skagway and panning for gold in 'Tent City'.

The agent told her about St. Michael's Russian Orthodox Church in Sitka, the Russian Dance Troupe in their beautiful costumes, and the legendary shops and stores of Juneau that were a 'must see'. She could hardly wait.

Her cruise was booked on the love-boat Princess and the time had already come for it. She was excited, and the boys were at the airport to see her off on the first leg of her journey.

She wistfully waved to them, wishing they could have come—in some ways—and glad to be on her own for her 'retreat' time by herself.

The stateroom assigned to her was one deck down. "Go down the stairs, cross the lounge, then take the right hallway and it will be just a few doors down that hallway, #234, M'am," the man had told her.

It was more spacious than Cathy had imagined. A private bathroom and shower, a dresser to unpack and put her clothes into, a large closet to hang her dresses, and two large single-size beds, one along the wall under the porthole and the other to the left of the cabin as you entered the door. She didn't know who her roommate would be as she hadn't yet shown up.

Having put her clothes, cosmetics, and suitcases away, and to officially begin her journey, Cathy had to watch the ship leave the dock. Hanging over the rail, she watched the dockhands toss off the cables, viewed the foamy water being stirred up by the propellers as they pushed the ship sideways away from the dock, and felt the vibration of the powerful engines in the deck beneath her feet. It gave her a thrill of expectation in the adventure she was embarking upon. It was the first time in almost twenty-four years she had been on her own, and alone, and she felt pangs of sadness for what was gone from her life.

The dining room that evening was crowded with a happy, laughing, cheerful crowd, all in the mood of beginning a new adventure. She found her assigned round table, #2, at the front of the room on the right side and as she was the first to arrive, chose a seat to be facing the room.

"Ah, M'am, the others will be joining you soon," the waiter said with a smile as he filled the water glasses.

"Am I too early?"

"No, they should all be arriving soon. Is there someone you particularly are waiting for, M'am?"

"No, I'm traveling alone this trip, I'm afraid."

It was only a few minutes before two couples arrived, bantering merrily, swiveling their heads back and forth to check everything and everyone. Seeing that 'yes-indeed, we-do-have-a-very-good-table, yes-indeedy' look on their faces, Cathy decided there really wouldn't be too much trouble with dinner conversation.

Joining the group lastly was a diminutive dapper young man in dress-white naval uniform. He introduced himself as Kenny, and his job was Second Officer of the ship, and explained to the people his home was in England, "London, ya' know." His delightful cockney accent and his physical appearance was immediately reminiscent of one of the famous foursome sons of that island and every one throughout dinner strained to hear his witty and softly spoken remarks.

His seat was next to Cathy, and his charm wrapped around her. He was very mindful and considerate of her, taking her under his wing to make sure she didn't feel like a fifth wheel being the only other single person at the table. And the meal was excellent, the waiters making it more fun with their singing, jokes, and the very efficient manner in which they served, somehow making each person feel special.

Sitting there with Kenny after the other couples had left the table to go to the lounge show, she was aware that he, also, was excusing himself, stating he 'had to go back to… where? She wasn't sure she had understood what he said, but it sounded like, 'the bridge'. Well, that did seem right.

"Please don't feel you have to sit with me, Kenny. I'm going to enjoy this iced tea and leave in a few minutes also. Please, it's all right, I'm fine," she urged him.

Cathy sat and gazed at the people still sitting at their tables, hearing the burst of hilarity now and then, the laughing faces bobbing up and down in animated conversations.

The man, sitting at the second table down the row in the middle of the room with his back to her, drew her attention.

He had the same bearing, sitting so straight and tall, as... oh boy, Cathy, you have had enough iced tea. What do they put into this drink if you're starting to see Joe in the straight back and broad shoulders of a stranger?

Quickly leaving the table, she headed for the lounge on the lower deck. A stage show was being presented and she might as well see all she can see and do all she can do.

She was very surprised at the end of the show to discover the players were all employees who held other jobs throughout the ship. Room attendants, food service, waiters, and mechanics, gift shop, and employees from all the services the ship had to offer. They worked very hard, and the show was professional in its glitzy and smashing presentation.

A beautiful night. Strolling along the decks, in and out of foyers and lounges, Cathy enjoyed the solitude. There were party's going on here and there, she was sure, but this was what she needed right now—peace, and the stars just beginning to show.

It was a late sunset, almost 10:15, and now at midnight the darkness of the water and sky blended together without a seam to separate them, and only a bright moon cast its glow across it.

The next day was charged with sights; the dazzling sun danced offthe water-caps as the ship plowed steadily on its course. Dolphins played alongside the ship, and seals rested on small ice floes, sliding angrily into the water as the ship disturbed their siesta.

It was warm enough for just a light covering outside, a sweater or such, and

Cathy strolled the decks again, becoming familiar with each, watching the waves and seeing the shoreline dip and turn in and out. It was calming, it was soothing, it was just what she needed. No conversational commitments except at mealtimes, and even breakfast and lunch could be by herself, if she wanted.

That evening the other couples had arrived at the table before she did, Kenny coming a little later when the salad was being served. He offered his apologies, "On duty and all, ya' know."

The man at the second table in the middle of the room was now facing toward Cathy. She glanced over at him and stopped in her tracks with her fork in midair. She forcibly kept herself from crying out. Her breath felt as if it was being shut off.

The similarity she perceived in this man when compared to her memory of Joe was astounding, her face turning white in her struggle to decide what to think. He was wearing glasses now, and she couldn't really see his eyes from this distance, she squinted as she tried, but the hair and facial contour looked to be the same; perhaps the hair a little more sparse, it was hard to tell from this distance.

"Hello, there, Mrs Mitchell, are you all right?" The concern in Kenny's voice was genuine. He had seen many passengers with seasickness, and they looked just the same as Cathy did at this moment.

"I'm fine, Kenny, really. But perhaps I will take my leave and have a snack later in my cabin." Her voice was shaky and tight. "Please, excuse me." She stood up and walked as elegantly as possible on weakened legs toward the entrance door.

It was at this moment the man looked up, catching the movement of a flashy red dress with a few sparkling sequins against the black uniforms of the waiters who were scurrying about, and, as she took one last glance at him from the doorway, dropped his silverware with a clatter onto his plate.

Her heart had skipped several beats in that parting glance.

There was a connection of some kind there! But surely, it had to be her vivid imagination coming into play. Surely...! It's too much to even speculate about. It is too much!

She didn't go to her cabin, but went out onto the deck and inhaled deeply of the air, trying to get her equilibrium back, trying to settle herself down, trying to convince herself she was a very silly woman letting her fantasy take too much hold on her.

Laughing to herself, wryly grinning and calling herself all kinds of foolish names, she relaxed and gazed around her. It was only a short while before people began coming out for a breather from dinner.

Ohmygod, there he is again.

Much closer now, he stepped over the raised threshold, turned to offer his hand to someone behind him. A left hand with a gold band adorning the fourth finger grasped his hand and stepped out onto the deck, a young man closely following her.

They were only a few dozen feet way.

Cathy gasped, Oh, my Lord. It is him. It is Joe! Up this close, I'd know that man anywhere, and the woman has to be his... wife, the young man... his son? But... he can't be. Oh, Lord, let me just curl up here and perish into these deck cracks! I can't let him see me. I can't!

In an almost hysterical state, she turned and walked the opposite direction from which they had turned. Rushing into and through the foyers, she went down one deck, crossed the lounge and into the hallway on the right, found her door, entered and slammed it closed behind her. She collapsed against the door onto the floor, her tears coming in anguished sobbing.

"Of all the places in the world, why here, why now, why? And he's married." Her cries of misery and heartbreak resounded in the close walls of her cabin.

Finally, ultimately, "I have to be very happy for him," she moaned.

The ship docked at Ketchikan the next day, and streams of tourists disembarked the ship to sightsee in the town, touring the fish hatchery and many places of interest. Cathy was supposed to be among them, but decided to stay on board keeping an eye out for any sign of an appearance of Joe and his family.

Her life was taken from her now, the desire to see and speak to him almost overwhelming. But the need to not upset his life was more prevailing in her heart. She had to stay out of his sight, out of his life, out of his arms. Or, am I presuming too much? Would he be as upset as I am? Would seeing me again cause any upheaval in his life? Don't be such a silly twit, she admonished, he has his family with him!

She stayed close to her cabin all day, only going to eat at one of the open buffets when most of the crowd had gone, scurrying back to the womb of her stateroom almost immediately.

In frantic haste the next morning she checked with the ships' purser; there was no way to get off the ship and go home. Transportation was available from some towns of Alaska, but with more expense than she could afford. No, I'll just have to tough it out, stay out of sight, and catch the air late at night when it's safer and not as many people are about. She worked desperately to compose herself, trying to come to terms with what was happening.

It is 1:20 in the morning, very late on this cooler night, and Cathy cannot rest, knows there is no rest until she is off this ship.

Ghostly puffs of the cooler late night breeze feel like lustrous black silk against her skin as they dance and play around her face and ankles. She leans heavily and very despondently against the railing as the ship rolls lightly in the gentle waves. She agonizes, leaning so hard against this railing could be such an easy answer. All I'd have to do would be to lean a little further over...!

Unnerving memories are strangling her, at times screaming to her, Jump... Jump... stop this torment! But the quiet inner voice of her soul overrides her screams and states, I can't do that.

But, she mused, to go overboard would be a sure thing. The icy water would not allow me to survive but a few minutes even if anyone knew I had jumped overboard. But I can't do that to my sons; what would they think of their mother doing that? No, hang tough, she pensively sighed, stay out of sight; stay away from the one person remaining in life who could make me happy and which cannot happen now.

She jumped apprehensively when a deep soft voice came out of the subdued darkness from close behind her.

"I missed seeing you at dinner." A very gentle, husky voice. "You were the brightest light within that dining room, and it was rather dull tonight. I wondered why until I looked toward your table and you weren't there."

She stiffened upright, but did not turn around, the purring sound of the voice causing thrills to chase up and down her spine. Then a tightness settled in her lower stomach with prickles rising on the back of her neck. Frozen, her hands gripped the rail until the knuckles were white even in the darkness.

With her heart beginning to race ever faster, "I beg your pardon? Are you speaking to me?" she asked.

His hoarsely whispered reply, "You know I am, Princess."

In her acknowledgement, panic rose in her voice , "Go away! Please, go away. I can't look at you, or see you, or be with you. You have your family with you."

She blurted out indignantly, "And how dare you come out here looking for me when you... you're...."

She couldn't go on, the tears were hot and stinging in her eyes, her breathing in jagged searing hot grunts of pain.

He breathed deeply. When he spoke his voice was shaking and trembling. "Yes, I have my family with me. My sister, who is a nun and I'm giving this trip to as a present for her thirtieth jubilee in the convent."

Another deep sigh. "And my brothers' son, my nephew, whom I'm giving this trip to as a college Masters' graduation present. Yep, they're my family all right," he breathed, "Couldn't imagine my life without them."

He dragged his breath in as if he were struggling against high winds, "Princess, I'm free of any entanglement, job-wise, or, otherwise. There is no one else in my life."

Stunned by his words she turned slowly toward him with downcast eyes, shaking her head in disbelief. She glanced quickly up to his face, then as quickly down. In a tense but firm voice, she told him, "I've been married, Joe. I have three almost grown sons."

"That's wonderful, Cathy." Then the edge of an angry-sounding growl was in his utterance of dismay, "I haven't seen anyone with you. Where's your husband and why isn't he with you?"

"He died several years ago. I'm widowed, Joe."

The hostile attitude in his temperament vanished instantly, "I'm so sorry, Cathy."

He hesitated for a moment longer, then reached into his dinner-jacket pocket and pulled out a small hard clear-plastic case. Reaching out toward her he opened it to display a tiny gold chain and gold heart locket.

"I've never forgotten you, my Princess. This is probably about the hundredth case I've had to use; they all kept wearing out."

She stared at the tiny case in his large manicured hand, then her eyes followed the crook of his arm up to his shoulder and across to his chin. She let her viewing continue to travel slowly up and toured his face. He had removed his glasses and moisture was glistening in his eyes.

She finally gazed as if in a mesmerized state into warm electric pools of blue; eyes that made her feel as if she could be inhaled deeply into them.

Joe replaced the case into his jacket pocket then reached out tentatively with both arms, and she unhesitatingly stepped into his cushioning embrace of velvet steel that no longer needed to be withheld from her for any job, for any reason. He was still ramrod straight, hard-muscled and strong, his military life indelibly impacted into him.

"Princess! Cathy!," his voice was muffled and purred against her cheek and hair.Over and over he breathed her name to her, and each time she heard him say her name, she fell more deeply into his spell, pressed more closely against his warm hard body as he pulled her ever closer. She could feel his heart race, and her own was pounding and singing, along with the blaring of the trumpets.

He took her upturned face between his hands, caressing her soft cheeks and touching still full lips with his thumbs. Cathy ran her tongue across those dry lips, and Joe felt an electric jolt pulse through him. Bending his head he kissed those tongue-moistened lips so gently. Within her closed watery eyes visions of soft white angelic creatures were floating round and round, gliding and dancing in and out of the mists singing his name over and over, "Joe..., Joe..., Joe...."

She then realized it was her voice singing his name out lovingly and low.Cathy responded as only one who was captured by the angels can, and both she and Joe were quickly quivering and pulsating, tasting, caressing, nuzzling. Each burning kiss pressed onto the other was a declaration of unconditional yielding.

Circling around her at touching closeness, he hugged and kissed her from every conceivable side, his hands softly stroking the silkiness of her arms, neck, cheeks, and sliding feather light under her cloak down to her waist and hips: love and desire was being rekindled with each kiss, each sensory nerve was being relit with fires that had been thought to be ash. They smiled into each others' eyes often.

He was here and hers; she was his; both knowing this without having to speak about it. Finally, someday soon, there would be more intermingling between them than just their happy tears.

There will be some other time to hear and tell the stories of their lives, and to introduce each other to their families.

Now, tonight, all they needed, or wanted, was for each to be alone with the other.

As strong as when it had budded into life that very first time so many years ago, now their longing for each other exploded into swift and full bloom. Each was lost to the other, and each sigh was joyful, rapturous surrender to a fully accepted burning love.

They finally embraced tightly in a bonding that would never be shattered again, and which the distance of time had not diminished.